"You're freezing," David said, standing close behind her. "I'll come in and build a fire."

In moments he'd arranged the dry logs, lined the kindling, and found the matches on top of the mantel. The tiny flame flared, then caught.

He stood to face her, his wet shirt hugging a very broad chest, his soaked jeans clinging to muscular thighs. She shivered. She hadn't seen that much man up close in years.

"You're still freezing," David said, wrapping his arms around her, bringing her close to the fire. She leaned into him, loving the way her wet body felt against his.

"Stay right here," he said. "Don't move." Before she knew it, he'd returned from the bathroom with towels, and without a word he began to dry her hair. Lifting damp strands of her hair, he rubbed them against the cloth, making her feel more cherished than she ever had. Everywhere he touched her she tingled with erotic pleasure. Then she felt the towels fall away, and David's fingers wove through her hair. She didn't know who made the first move, but suddenly they were in each other's arms, wet and wild and hungry. . . .

WHAT ARE *LOVESWEPT* ROMANCES?

They are stories of true romance and touching emotion. We believe those two very important ingredients are constants in our highly sensual and very believable stories in the *LOVESWEPT* line. Our goal is to give you, the reader, stories of consistently high quality that may sometimes make you laugh, sometimes make you cry, but are always fresh and creative and contain many delightful surprises within their pages.

Most romance fans read an enormous number of books. Those they truly love, they keep. Others may be traded with friends and soon forgotten. We hope that each *LOVESWEPT* romance will be a treasure—a "keeper." We will always try to publish

LOVE STORIES YOU'LL NEVER FORGET
BY AUTHORS YOU'LL ALWAYS REMEMBER

The Editors

Peggy Webb

The Edge of Paradise

BANTAM BOOKS

NEW YORK · TORONTO · LONDON · SYDNEY · AUCKLAND

THE EDGE OF PARADISE
A Bantam Book / December 1992

If you would be interested in receiving protective vinyl
covers for your Loveswept books, please write to this address
for information:

Loveswept
Bantam Books
P.O. Box 985
Hicksville, NY 11802

ISBN 0-553-44200-7

Published simultaneously in the United States and Canada

Bantam Books are published by Bantam Books, a division of
Bantam Doubleday Dell Publishing Group, Inc. Its trademark,
consisting of the words "Bantam Books" and the portrayal of
a rooster, is Registered in U.S. Patent and Trademark Office
and in other countries. Marca Registrada. Bantam Books, 666
Fifth Avenue, New York, New York 10103.

PRINTED IN THE UNITED STATES OF AMERICA
OPM   0 9 8 7 6 5 4 3 2 1

Acknowledgment

The author gratefully acknowledges the help of Dennis Bailey, a native son of Tupelo, Mississippi, who is one of opera's great baritones.

One

"The trouble with Widow Brown is those clothes she wears."

At the sound of her name, Rosalie Brown stopped her grocery cart in the canned-fruit section and peered between the peaches and the apricots. Her former next-door neighbor, Grace Crowley, was talking to the town gossip, Mildred Martin.

"I know just what you mean," Mildred said. "Red, for goodness' sake. And with sequins, even in the daytime. Whoever heard of a grieving widow wearing sequins?"

Rosalie touched the shoulder of her jumpsuit. Sequins. And the suit was red.

"Sequins. At her age," Grace said. "Imagine that."

Rosalie didn't happen to think thirty-six was all that old. And anyhow, Grace was one to talk. She was pushing forty herself, and the whole town knew she still stuffed her size-fourteen behind into a size-twelve slacks.

Rosalie stood in the aisle, undecided. The smart thing to do would be to move on. Let the biddies cluck. Words couldn't hurt her. On the other hand, she was curious about what they would say next.

"If you ask me," Mildred said, "the trouble with Widow Brown is that she doesn't appear to be grieving."

Rosalie clutched the handle of her cart, too mad to move on. *Why should I grieve?* she wanted to shout. *I didn't even like Harry, let alone love him.* She had loved him once. Madly. But many small and subtle cruelties had killed that, long before Harry had died.

"I'll say she's not. She's too busy frittering away his property. Lost Harry's house, and his car to boot. And him not cold in his grave."

Harry had been cold in the grave for six months, as everybody in Tupelo well knew. One of life's great ironies to Rosalie was that the thing she loved most about the town was also the thing she hated most: Everybody kept up with everybody else. In times of need, word spread quickly, and the townspeople gathered round. Word also spread quickly of alleged misdoings, and many were ready to cast stones.

As for frittering away his property—Harry's debts had more than equaled his estate. The house, the car, and most of the savings had gone to pay off his creditors.

She forced her hands to relax. No use getting upset over something as insignificant as grocery-store gossip. Not when she had bigger worries, such as how she would pay her rent and how she would keep her sons, Jack and Jimmy, in college.

Rosalie lifted her chin and pushed her cart up the aisle. The battle of life had left her battered and bruised, but she wasn't down yet, not by a long shot. She would walk over hot coals before she'd let anybody think she was defeated. And it looked as if she was going to have to, for Mildred and Grace were congregated at the end of the aisle, blocking the way to the cereals.

Rosalie put on her perkiest grin. "Hello, Mildred . . . Grace. Isn't this a beautiful day for grocery shopping?"

"That's just what I was saying to Grace," Mildred said. "A beautiful day for shopping."

Rosalie kept her smile in place. "There's nothing like a little nip in the air to make a body feel good."

"And how are you feeling, dear?" Grace arranged her face in all the downward angles appropriate for condolence. Rosalie would laugh about it when she got in her secondhand car. "Poor Harry. Dead and gone."

"Life goes on," Rosalie said, managing to keep a straight face as she spouted the platitude. Then she gave them a jaunty wave and headed down the aisle for cereal. She was usually careful to select the cheapest brand, but today she grabbed the first box she could get her hands on—high-priced natural cereal, full of things that were supposed to be good for her.

She hurried her cart around the corner, keeping up her sprightly walk until she was out of sight of Mildred and Grace. Then she allowed herself to slump. The cereal box accused her from the cart.

Nearly five dollars. It must be filled with gold shavings. Rosalie took one step backward and peered up the cereal aisle. Mildred and Grace looked as if they had taken up residence there, standing with their carts glued together, talking as fast and hard as they could, both moving their mouths at the same time.

Rosalie straightened her shoulders and moved on to the checkout line. It was too late to put the cereal back. If she waited until they left, she might be late to her evening job. And she couldn't afford to lose one of her jobs.

She'd just have to do without hamburger this week and tell herself the cereal was a nice change.

The house was in a neighborhood that had once been smart. David Kelly stood on the cracked sidewalk admiring the small touches of fading elegance—a stained-glass upstairs window set in the peeling clapboard walls of the house next door, one Corinthian column intact on the front porch of the house across the street, the beautiful curving bay window of his own house.

He walked up his creaking steps, fitted the key into the rusty lock of his new rental house, and went inside. Sunshine coming through the dirty windows picked up cobwebs in the corners and dust motes in the air.

"Home, sweet home," he said.

He set his duffel bags down and surveyed his new home. The couch sagged, the chair looked like a home for mice, and the desk by the corner was propped up with a brick under one leg. He had lived in worse.

Anyhow, surroundings didn't matter to him. Possessions didn't matter. Nothing much mattered except getting through each day with as little personal pain as possible. And getting through with a certain *joie de vivre*.

David made a quick tour of the rest of the house. It would do. It had a bed, a stove, a bathroom, hot and cold running water. It had an old furnace that looked in working order and a big oscillating fan to keep him cool in the summer.

From his dusty bedroom window he had a view of the house next door as well as shade from the sprawling oak tree that grew at the back corner of his house. A few acorns hit the roof with a plop, and a gray squirrel scampered down the tree trunk.

"My very own entertainment." David smiled as the squirrel retrieved his acorns and hurried back up the tree.

He watched the squirrel for a while longer, then unzipped a duffel bag and set about stowing his meager possessions.

The labored sound of a car engine brought David to his window. He wiped away a layer of dust on the windowpane and looked toward the house next door. The car pulling into the driveway was ancient, a 1973 Chevrolet that had once been gold. Now it was rusty in spots and faded a dull yellow in others. Smoke puffed up from the hood when it stopped.

"Running hot," he said. Of course, that was not his concern. And he certainly didn't plan to make it his business.

The car door opened on the driver's side, and he saw the legs first—long, slender, encased in red.

"Turn away, fool," he whispered. But he didn't pay himself any attention.

A woman emerged from the car. The first thing David noticed was the sequins. Row upon shining row of them decorated the front of her jumpsuit. The sun reflected off them and sent a sparkling rainbow across the woman's face. It was not a beautiful face by ordinary standards. It was not even a pretty face in the classical manner. But it was an arresting face, an intriguing face. Her mouth was wide, her nose was small and uptilted, and her eyes looked too big for her face.

The woman bent down and lifted two paper bags from the car. She was graceful and curving from waist to ankle. Womanly. Tempting, even.

Abruptly, David left the window. But not before he

noticed her hair. It was not blond, not brown, not red, but an interesting combination of all three. And it bounced when she walked.

He ached a little when he turned away, then forced himself to whistle. He was in a new house, a new town. Memories would fade.

With determined steps he took his private stash of peanut butter and crackers from his duffel bag and carried them into the kitchen. A snack was just the thing he needed.

He spread peanut butter on two crackers, squashed them together, and ate with gusto.

"Pure protein," he said. He took one bite, then wandered over to the window. The woman was in her kitchen, unloading groceries. Without meaning to spy, David stood at his window watching.

She moved with grace and determination and purpose. He admired her from the safety of his kitchen.

With nothing separating the houses except a narrow driveway, David was close enough to see most of the things she took from her bag. The other things he could guess.

She stowed her milk and eggs in the refrigerator, then dragged a stool across the floor and climbed up to stow her cereal. She was not a tall woman, and her cabinets, if they were like the ones in his house, were built too high for convenience.

"Damned fool thing to do," he muttered. "Putting the cereal out of reach." She'd have to climb the stool every time she wanted a bowlful.

It was none of his business. He left the window and wandered through his house, whistling his hollow tune. As if some invisible string were pulling him, he occasionally glanced at his windows.

The woman was moving through her house, too, pausing every now and then to do little things women who loved their houses often did: She straightened a picture on the wall, picked up a magazine and moved it from one table to another, repositioned an afghan on the back of a rocking chair.

David wandered closer to his window, not spying, not hiding, but staying back in the shadows so he wouldn't be seen. No use advertising that he was in town. He was a loner, and that's the way he wanted to keep it.

The woman's phone rang, and he could see her in three-quarter profile as she talked. Her face became animated, even beautiful. Who had caused that change in her? A dear friend? A husband? A lover?

Before he could speculate further, she hung up and left the room. David moved through his house, aimlessly, he told himself, not following her. Both of them ended up in their respective bedrooms.

He could see her back and a reflection from her mirror. She reached for the zipper on her jumpsuit. David hesitated only a moment, then wheeled and left his room. There was a thin line between curiosity and dangerous fascination—and he had almost crossed it.

Taking his tools, he went into his backyard. There was always something in need of repair around old houses, and he definitely needed to have a hammer in his hand.

He glanced at the house next door. The woman had pulled down her bedroom shades. He was glad. It wasn't wise for any woman to undress with her shades up—no matter how safe she thought her neighborhood was.

He found the back-porch steps sagging. Grateful, he pulled out hammer and nails and set to work. The sounds of his carpentry rang out on the crisp autumn air. His mind shut out everything except the exact angle of the nail and the precision of the hammer blows.

"Excuse me."

At the sound of the woman's voice, his hammer glanced off the nail and banged against the wooden step.

"Dammit," he said automatically, looking up. The woman from next door stood watching him. She had changed out of her jumpsuit into a uniform of some kind, pink with a short fitted skirt and button-up blouse. She wore shoes without heels, but her legs still looked great.

David quickly looked away. He would concentrate on something else—her eyes. They were blue. Actually, they were a remarkable shade of blue, not quite green and not quite violet, but an astonishing mixture of the two. The artist in him appreciated her eyes. Not to mention the chained but untamed beast in him.

"I'm sorry. I didn't mean to startle you."

"It's nothing."

"You just moved in." It was not a question.

"Yes."

"I saw you on the way to my car, and I thought I'd better come over and explain things."

"What things?" he asked, merely for the sake of politeness. He didn't want this enticing woman with the lovely eyes and lovely legs to explain things to him. He wanted to be left alone.

"First, let me introduce myself. I'm Rosalie Brown."

She held out her hand. What could he do but take it?

"David Kelly," he said, noticing how soft her hand was. She shook his in a firm and businesslike manner, then let go. He felt an inward sag of relief, almost as if he had been rescued. But how could he be rescued when he had never been threatened? He might think about it later. Or he might not. He might just read a good book instead.

"Welcome to the neighborhood, David."

"Thanks."

What was she? The official welcoming committee? He wished she would leave. Her smile was lovely, and she had an unsettling way of looking at him, as if she saw beyond the surface.

"What I wanted to tell you is that we share a driveway . . . but then I guess Mr. Winston explained that to you when he rented the house."

"He didn't."

"He's old and sometimes forgetful."

Rosalie fiddled with the ribbon holding back her hair. The sun glinted on the underside of her arms. They were soft and creamy and vulnerable, laced with a tiny network of blue veins. He was glad when she stopped arranging her hair, for the sight of her soft arms did something strange to him: It set up longings he hadn't had in a long time.

"Anyhow," she said, "we *do* share the driveway, and I thought I'd find out what your working hours are so I won't block you in." She paused, waiting. When he didn't say anything, she spoke again. "Or we could exchange car keys. . . . That's what I did with the last person who lived here. That way, we wouldn't have to worry about getting blocked in."

"I don't have a car."

"Oh . . . I'm sorry."

"No need to be sorry. I don't need a car; therefore, I don't have one." He sounded like a pompous ass, even to himself. Maybe she would leave.

He thought about the blue veins on the undersides of her arms. His hand tightened on the hammer.

"Well . . ." Rosalie smiled brightly. "That takes care of that." She smoothed down her skirt. He noticed how trim her legs were. "I'd better leave, or I'll be late for work. Nice meeting you."

"Same here," he said, redeeming himself, he guessed. Or maybe not. It wasn't much of a reply. And she *had* been friendly. Not flirtatious. Not effusive or pushy or nosy. Just friendly.

He thought he might say something else, but she was already at her car. He'd have to shout in order to be heard. It didn't seem to be worth the trouble.

Her old car backfired, then caught. She saw him watching her and waved through the window. Rosalie Brown seemed like a nice woman. He hoped Mr. Brown appreciated her. If there was a Mr. Brown. He hadn't asked, hadn't really wanted to know.

David took up his hammer and began to swing at a nail. Metal connecting with metal made a satisfying sound.

She hadn't been wearing a ring. He'd noticed that. The only jewelry she'd worn was a watch, the inexpensive kind you could buy in any discount store.

She'd worn fingernail polish. Red. Chipped on the right index finger. He found that chipped red polish brave and somehow endearing.

Sweat popped out on his brow, although the weather was brisk and a breeze stirred the branches of the oak tree where the gray squirrel chattered. He wiped at the sweat and kept on hammering.

The top button of her blouse had been open, exposing the petal-soft skin of her neck and throat. There had been a hint of blue veins there, too, just on the side of her throat. She had the kind of fair skin that made her look delicate and vulnerable— whether she was or not. For all he knew, she could be a cold, tough number. But he didn't think so. His training plus the gut instinct that had served him well for twenty-odd years on the police force told him Rosalie Brown was a warm, generous-hearted woman making it in the world, with or without a man.

He swung the hammer, satisfied with the solid blows he landed on the nails, pleased with the improved sturdiness of the steps. The squirrel scampered by, scolding.

David smiled. Then he thought of the lettering on Rosalie Brown's pink blouse. THE EDGE OF PARADISE. It was probably the name of some small café, or even a nightclub, where she worked. The lettering had been done with bright blue thread in Old English script.

Sweat popped out on his face again. He sat back on his heels, thinking of the words, not bothering to wipe the sweat away. The edge of paradise. He had been there once. He didn't plan to go again.

Two

The Edge of Paradise was an aging wooden café hunkered down between two ultramodern high-rise office buildings. With its green glass windows and its fifty years of accumulated paint, peeling in layers so it looked spotted, it always put Rosalie in mind of an old hound dog, hairless and toothless but still faithful and willing to serve.

The café was a landmark in Tupelo, a beloved tradition. Every time progress threatened it, concerned citizens rallied to save it. A yellowing Save-the-Paradise flyer was still taped to the west window.

Big Betty Malone, the owner of the café, never got in a hurry about anything. The ancient flyer, along with an accumulation of outdated calendars on the walls and the Christmas wreath that hung behind the cash register year round, attested to her slow-moving ways.

That was one of the things Rosalie liked best about working at the Edge of Paradise, the relaxed pace. That, and the owner herself. Big Betty doted on Rosalie, and the feeling was mutual.

"If you ain't a sight for sore eyes," Big Betty yelled

when Rosalie walked through the door, as if she hadn't seen her in years instead of over the past week. "Come here and give us a little hug."

Big Betty folded Rosalie in a warm embrace. Her hugs had sustained Rosalie through the lean years of raising two boys alone, and later through the endless days of Harry's illness. Cancer. Death by inches.

"You're getting skinny, honey." Betty held her at arm's length for inspection. "You eating enough?"

"Don't you worry. If I ate any more, they'd have to declare me a state and parcel me out for homesteading." Rosalie thought of the overpriced cereal sitting in her cabinet, depriving her of at least two good chopped steaks. Why hadn't she just put it back on the shelf beside the tartar sauce and the ketchup?

Because she always tried to do the right thing. That's why.

She tied on a white ruffled apron, picked up a damp cloth, and began to scrub the pink Formica tabletops. Sometimes she wished she were the kind of woman who would pack her red high heels and her sequined jumpsuit, then get all her money out of savings and run off to San Francisco or New York or even New Jersey, for goodness' sake, instead of the kind who always stayed home to take care of everybody else.

Sometimes. But not often. She had two fine sons, good friends, enough money to keep body and soul together. What more could a woman want?

Betty took up a flat-bladed spatula and began to scrape the griddle. "What's new?" she called over the racket.

"I have a new neighbor. David Kelly."

"Irish, huh?"

"I guess." Rosalie thought of his blue eyes and thick dark hair. "Yes, I think so."

"What's he like?"

"It was hard to tell. He didn't say much."

"Not very friendly, huh?"

Rosalie remembered the quiet strength of David Kelly, the way he had seemed a part of his backyard, as if he were one of the great oaks that had grown there.

"He was just reserved," she said, defending him without understanding why. "Maybe he's the quiet type, or he could be shy."

She didn't think so, though. He had studied her with a directness that had been almost disconcerting, not in the way of a man who undresses a woman with his eyes but in the way of a man who wanted to discover who she was.

"Anyway," she added, "friendly doesn't always mean nice." Take Harry, for instance. There hadn't been a more sociable man in town than Harry Brown. And look where that had led. To a marriage made in hell.

"You're right. Why, I'd a' thought the way Harry came in here courting you, he was God's gift to widows and orphans. And look what a lowdown skunk he turned out to be."

Sometimes Rosalie thought Betty could read her mind.

The cowbell on the front door created a racket as six young people entered the café, and it was soon lively with the sounds of happy conversation and laughter.

Time passed quickly for Rosalie, as it always did at the café. She took orders with an efficiency born of long experience while laughing and chatting with customers, calling most of them by name.

Behind her, the cowbell jangled almost constantly.

"Rosalie, table one," Big Betty yelled.

"Coming."

She hurried toward the table, writing her last order as she walked. Almost there, she looked up, straight into the faces of her twin sons.

"Surprise!" they yelled at the same time. Both of them came around the table and hugged her, Jimmy on the left side and Jack on the right.

"We'll have hamburgers and a hug, Mom," Jack said, laughing. "Heavy on the hugs."

"Why didn't you tell me you were coming?" She squeezed and patted and hugged. "Just look at you. Are you eating enough? Are your classes hard? Do your teachers appreciate your brilliance?" She hugged and patted some more. "It's been so long."

"Yeah, Mom," Jimmy said. "Three whole weeks."

"It seems like an eternity. How did you get here?"

"Caught a ride with Shine Jenkins. He's home for the weekend." Jack took her hand and urged her into a chair. "Sit down a minute, Mom. You don't need to be on your feet so much."

"For just a minute, honey." Rosalie swallowed a big lump that came into her throat. How like his father Jack was. Always worrying about her, always petting her. He even looked like his father, big, stocky, dark-haired and dark-eyed.

Joe Mack Westmoreland rose bright in her vision, laughing, calling her his songbird. The memories of their young love had sustained her for years after his death, and now, even after the awful interlude with Harry, she was reaching back to those ancient memories, using them to remind herself that love between a man and a woman *did* exist, and that it was capable of thriving against all the odds.

Rosalie blinked at the sudden moisture in her eyes. Jack draped his arm across her shoulders. "Visiting with ghosts again, Mom?"

"Only one."

Big Betty brought a platter of hamburgers to the

table. "You don't mind if I join you, do you?" She scooted in beside Jimmy, certain of her welcome. "There's nothing I like more than being seen with the two best-looking men in Tupelo."

In the company of her dear sons and her best friend, Rosalie reminded herself how lucky she was. What did it matter that the pillow on the other side of her bed remained undented, that the part of herself she knew existed, that hot, sweet core of passion, had been in hibernation for years?

She had her sons; she had her friends.

While they ate, Jack and Jimmy kept Rosalie and Betty laughing with their exaggerated tales of college life. Rosalie laughed loudest of all. Then those fine young men, the joy of her life, tied on aprons and helped her wait tables.

Around nine-thirty, when the noise from the café crowd had settled down to a contented hum, Betty urged Rosalie and her boys out the door.

"I can't leave you with this crowd," Rosalie said. "It's two hours to closing."

"Go home and enjoy your boys. If the day ever comes when Big Betty can't handle a Friday-night crowd, that's the day I take down the Christmas wreath and close the doors."

Grateful, Rosalie climbed in the front seat between her sons. Jack took the wheel and Jimmy spun yarns that had them laughing all the way home.

David was sitting on his sagging sofa reading Wordsworth when he heard Rosalie's car. There was no mistaking the labored clunking of the engine. He glanced at his watch. Almost ten o'clock. Not too late, but with an old car like that, it was damned late enough.

He laid his book on the sofa and was halfway to the window before he checked himself.

"Fool," he muttered. "She's no concern of yours."

The beautiful lyric poetry of Wordsworth captured his attention for all of five seconds, and then he heard the voices. Male voices. Not one but two.

What was this Rosalie Brown? A party girl? She hadn't looked the type.

He listened to the sounds of male laughter. What did it matter what she was? He reread the first line of *The Prelude*, tracing it with his finger, trying to concentrate.

"Hey, Mom?" The voice rang out on the still night air, clearly defining Rosalie's relationship with the young men. David felt a foolish sense of relief. "How long since you've been dancing?"

"Dancing?" Her laughter was clear and melodious. "I've probably forgotten how."

"What do you say, Jim? Shall we give her a refresher course?"

"Yeah. How about it, Mom?"

Doors slammed, shutting off the laughter and Rosalie's reply. David felt deprived. He sat in the stillness for a while, with nothing to cheer him except the book open on his lap and the feeble light from the overhead bulb cutting through the gloom.

Then he heard the music.

Getting up—to stretch his legs, he told himself—he wandered over to the window. Rosalie's house was alive with lights and music and movement. Two strapping young men took turns whirling her around her den.

She looked too young to be their mother. But there was no mistaking the relationship. One of them had her coloring, and both of them had her smile. It was a wide, genuine smile that lit the whole face.

David stood in the shadows of his curtains watching. The faint strains of their music echoed through his silent house, and the imagined lilt of their laughter echoed through his empty heart. He was watching love. And it was heartbreakingly beautiful. How long since he had known love, since he had felt the quiet jubilation of reciprocal affection?

The music played on. They danced, Rosalie and her sons. David clung to the shadows, unwilling to move away.

It was kind of nice, listening to music again.

The best of times always had a way of flying by, as if they were a holiday film on fast-forward.

Sunday afternoon Rosalie stood in her kitchen looking at three pieces of apple pie. That was all she had left of her weekend with Jack and Jimmy. They had caught a ride back to school earlier in the afternoon, taking cookies she had baked and doughnuts Betty had packed, taking their duffel bags and their liveliness and their laughter.

And now she was alone . . . with three pieces of pie.

A bird called from the nearby tree. She looked out the window and saw David Kelly in his backyard again, bent over his carpentry, his shirt damp with sweat. He was banging away with his hammer.

Not that the noise bothered her. On the contrary. She found his presence somehow comforting, though she couldn't explain why.

Leaning on her windowsill, she watched him awhile longer.

David paused in his work and turned to watch the gray squirrel gathering nuts under the oak tree. He smiled at the squirrel's antics, and so did she. From her vantage point in the kitchen, Rosalie felt almost as if she were sharing a quiet moment of pleasure with David.

Lord, she was fantasizing now, inventing secret pleasures for herself with someone who barely knew she existed. If she hadn't known she was totally in control of her faculties, totally capable of taking care of herself and two fine sons no matter what the circumstances, she might have worried about her sanity.

David's attention suddenly shifted, and he was watching her.

Caught spying. She felt foolish.

Turning quickly away, she hurried across her kitchen. As she passed the table, she spotted the pie, three uneaten pieces with nobody there to share it.

A wave of loneliness hit her so fast and so hard she had to blink back tears. *Joe Mack, why couldn't you have lived to share it all? Why couldn't you be here to save me from spying out the windows at a man who makes me wish for more than I have? Why couldn't you have lived to save me from Harry and a house not my own and three lonely pieces of pie?*

In that one unguarded moment the past overtook the present, and Rosalie stood in her kitchen feeling sorry for herself. She hated self-pity. If she didn't do something about it, the next thing she knew, she'd be on a crying jag.

Without thinking, she jerked up the pie and marched out her back door. David Kelly was still watching her house. Hot color flushed her cheeks as she continued her neighborly mission.

"Hello," she called, as if he didn't already see her, as if he weren't studying her with eyes so impossibly blue and clear, they made her head swim. If she had remembered how penetrating those eyes were, she might have stayed at home.

But it was too late now. She was already in his backyard, holding on to the pie.

"Hello," he said, leaving her to make all the conversation.

"I thought you might need some homemade pie."

A half-smile played around his lips, and she realized how foolish *that* sounded. She was so out of touch with the male-female connection that she felt as tongue-tied as a teenager.

"Not that you look undernourished or anything," she amended, looking him up and down and making things worse. He was a solid, muscular man, the kind who looked as if he'd be nice to lean on.

"My sons were home from college this weekend, you see, and you know how boys eat. . . ." She paused, wishing she didn't have her hands full so she could retie the hair ribbon she felt sagging against her neck, wishing she could disappear down an ant hole and pull the dirt in behind her, wishing to be anywhere in the world except standing in David Kelly's backyard enduring the solemn regard of his astonishing eyes.

Suddenly, he smiled. It was an unexpectedly wonderful smile, full of genuine compassion and open friendliness. Rosalie's hands relaxed on the pie plate. After all, she was glad she had come.

"I heard your music," he said. "Friday night."

"You did?"

"Yes."

For a moment his face was naked, his eyes bleak, and she felt as if her soul had touched his. But the moment passed quickly.

"I hope the noise didn't bother you," she said. "Things tend to get a little rowdy when the boys come home."

"It was a nice change."

"Yes, it *was* nice for a change."

"I don't take the time for music much anymore."

"Neither do I."

The unexpected confessions tumbled from them like a too-tight, too-hot blanket that had suddenly been kicked to the floor. In the quick, refreshing rush of truth, their gazes met, and their souls touched once more.

Rosalie's hand tightened on the pie plate. The hammer slid from David's hand and landed with a soft *thunk* on the ground. She thought he leaned toward her, just a little, as if he wanted to touch, needed the contact.

The silence stretched between them, breathless and full of possibilities. Then David looked away from her—deliberately, it seemed—and lifted the hammer once more.

She was being foolish, assigning her own feelings to him. It was she who needed the contact, she who craved the touch.

"I'll leave the pie here," she said, bending down to set the pie plate on a plank resting across the sawhorse. "I don't want to keep you from your work."

Rosalie had one last glimpse of his haunted eyes before she spun around to leave.

"Wait," David called.

Why should she wait? There was nothing there for her except one-sided conversation and a man who reminded her all too vividly that she was lonely.

"Don't go." His request sounded almost intimate, seductive.

Rosalie turned slowly, knowing her imagination was working overtime, knowing she should keep walking, but unable to do anything except stay.

"I didn't thank you for the pie," he said. "It was very kind of you to bring it over."

"It would have gone to waste."

He picked up the pie plate and sniffed. "It smells good."

"Homemade pies are my specialty. I learned the trick from Betty Malone, at the café where I work weekends."

"The Edge of Paradise?" She must have shown her surprise, for he added quickly, "I saw the lettering on your uniform."

That he had paid close attention to her and re- membered small details made her feel cared for in subtle ways she couldn't think about right now. *The mysteries of the human heart.* Who was she, of all people, to understand?

"And what do you do weekdays?" David asked, as if he were genuinely interested.

"I'm legal secretary for Mackey, Mahoney, and Bradford." There was a waiting stillness in him that made her add, "It's not what I set out to do many years ago, but it's where I ended up."

"Dreams rarely come true."

The demons that seemed to haunt this quiet, watchful man peered at her once more from his eyes. And then he smiled, banishing them to some private part of himself.

"Anyhow, thank you very much for the pie."

It was a dismissal. Rosalie left without saying good-bye. She merely smiled and waved, then turned and went back to her house.

Inside, she leaned against her doorframe, feeling flushed and out of breath. Even though she was approaching the downside of the hill by some peo- ple's standards, she certainly was not so out of shape that a brisk walk across the yard put her in that condition. No, it wasn't her walk that had her breathless: It was David Kelly.

In one brief encounter she had confessed that her life was without music and without dreams. And all because she had seen the private torment in his eyes.

And what do you do, David Kelly? Pounding ceaselessly with your hammer and nails?

He hadn't told her, and she hadn't asked. She didn't know whether she had been more afraid to ask or more afraid to know.

Harry had seemed to be a nice, kind man until she got to know him. She didn't think she could survive looking beneath any more facades and discovering the devil.

It was time to go to work.

Rosalie put aside thoughts of her mysterious neighbor and dressed for another Sunday-night stint at the Edge of Paradise.

After she left his backyard, David stood looking at the pie. The faint scent of cinnamon tickled his nostrils. His mouth watered for a taste of home cooking, and yet he couldn't bring himself to take a bite of Rosalie's offering.

He remembered the way she had looked, standing in his yard with her honey-and-cinnamon hair coming loose from its ribbon. She had been lovely and inviting in a way that had twisted his heart . . . and loosened his tongue.

His ill-timed confession about the music taunted him. For a man determined to be alone, he had made a mistake. Confession. Whoever said it was good for the soul?

The scent of cinnamon teased him. No use letting the pie go to waste. David picked it up and carried it inside.

He got a fork from his scant supply of eating utensils, then sat at the table, eating directly from the pie plate.

His second mistake with Rosalie was even worse than his first. Asking her personal questions. He didn't want to know about her private life. He didn't want to *care* about her broken dreams.

But he did. Dammitall, he did.

With her lovely eyes, her soft, lilting voice, and her home-baked pie, she had opened a tiny crack in his heavily armored heart and wedged herself in.

David sighed. Maybe he should get a dog. Two years was a long time to be alone.

Three

David always woke up early. It was a lifelong habit of his that had survived a disastrous marriage to a woman who cursed the morning sun, as well as a long stint on the night shift with the Red Bay, Alabama, police department.

As he stood in his kitchen, sipping his strong coffee and eating the last of the apple pie, he looked across the way. Rosalie was dragging a chair across her kitchen floor to her cabinet shelves.

David grinned. "I knew she'd have to climb up every time she wanted a bowl of cereal."

Setting his coffee aside, he leaned on his windowsill, watching. There was nothing groggy and sluggish about Rosalie Brown at six o'clock in the morning. With energetic, precise movements she mounted the chair and reached into the cabinet for her cereal. A short pink gown and robe swirled around her legs.

"She likes pink," David said, then he realized he was talking to himself. A dangerous habit. He definitely needed a dog.

He studied Rosalie, undetected. Her gown looked

soft to the touch, soft and silky. And under-neath . . . Would she be soft and silky too? Would her feminine curves fit his cupped hands? Would she be relaxed and languorous when he touched her, or would she be tight and hot and sexy?

Suddenly, Rosalie turned on her chair and looked straight at him. David broke into a sweat, as if she could read his mind.

Trapped, she stood on her chair, and he stood at the window. The sweat inched down the side of David's face as they stared at each other. Finally, Rosalie smiled and lifted her head in greeting, break-ing the spell that bound them.

He nodded his head and gave her the briefest of salutes, then turned quickly and left the kitchen. He didn't stop until he had gone into a small room on the far side of his house, as far away from Rosalie as he could get. It was an unfurnished room full of cobwebs and dust.

David waited in the dust, not hiding, merely avoid-ing that long, hard fall into sweet temptation.

He had fallen once, after long years of a loveless marriage, after the loneliness had eaten away his soul until he didn't think there was anything left. He had fallen so hard that he had broken all the rules. The result had been disaster—and a scar so deep, it had ripped out his heart.

Sweating, praying, clenching his fists so hard, the skin felt as if it would crack, David waited in the unused room until he heard the sound of Rosalie's car leaving the driveway. Only then did he come out.

He showered, dressed, then went to his back porch to gather the things he had made in the last three days. It was time to earn a few bucks. Just enough so he could keep on running.

• • •

Randy Prescott, owner of the Puss 'N Boots Pet Shop, looked at the array of birdhouses and doghouses spread out for his inspection. They were beautifully crafted, the woodwork smooth and the paint elegant. They looked more like the work of an artist than a carpenter.

"I'll take them all, Mr. Kelly."

"It's a deal." David Kelly pocketed the money Randy handed him.

"This is good work, better than factory-made." Randy lifted a birdhouse to inspect it closer. "Would you be interested in supplying these to me on a regular basis?"

David didn't want anything to tie him down to a certain schedule, a certain town. And yet, he had to eat. His savings wouldn't last forever.

"I can supply you as long as I'm in town," he said.

"And how long will that be, Mr. Kelly?"

Until I decide it's time to go, David thought, but didn't say it. "At least the rest of this month." His rent was paid up that long.

"A vagabond, huh?" Randy Prescott said, smiling.

"You could say that." Though it was far too glamorous a description of the way David's life felt to him.

"Then we have a deal." Randy offered his hand. "I'll buy everything you make for as long as you're in town. All I ask is that you let me know when you decide to leave."

"Done."

After David left the pet shop, he walked five blocks to the animal shelter to see if he could find a companion. The pedigreed black Labs in the pet shop had taken his eye, especially the one that kept thumping his tail, but David had far more in common with the misfits at the dog pound.

He selected a small brown dog with floppy ears, a sad face, and a long pink tongue that constantly licked his hand.

It was the next-best thing to love, and not nearly as risky.

Rover, he called the dog.

He and Rover were sitting side by side on his front porch steps, enjoying the late afternoon breeze, when Rosalie's old car came up the street. Coming home from work, he supposed.

He started to get up and go inside but then decided she had probably already seen him, and he didn't want to look as if he was avoiding her.

The car coughed to a stop, and Rosalie got out, smiling and waving. David thought to wave back, then vanished into his house, but Rover had other ideas. He dashed down the steps and began to lick Rosalie's legs.

Lucky dog.

"You precious little thing." Heedless of her skirt and stockings, Rosalie squatted beside the dog and began to pat his head. "You sweet old cuddlebum." Laughing, she scratched under his chin.

One of the ways David had always judged women was by how well they liked children and dogs. His ex-wife, Gretchen, had liked neither. That should have tipped him off.

"Is he yours?" Rosalie looked up at him, smiling.

"Yes. Got him today."

"What's his name?"

"I call him Rover, but he seems to like sweet old cuddlebum better. He's never licked my legs like that."

"Oh . . ." Rosalie stood up, reaching for the ribbon in her hair that wasn't there. "Well . . . my goodness." She actually seemed to be blushing. A woman her age. It was extraordinarily refreshing. "I'm just a sucker for babies and dogs," she said. "I always meant to have a houseful . . . of both."

That's when David knew he was in real trouble. He glanced around his porch, but there was no way to escape without seeming cowardly and obvious. Besides that, he didn't want to hurt Rosalie's feelings.

"Do you and Mr. Brown have children besides the twins?" A funny look crossed her face. "Your boys are fraternal twins, aren't they? They seem to enjoy the special camaraderie of twins."

"Yes, they're twins." She licked her lips. "But not Mr. Brown's. My boys belong to my first husband. Joe Mack Westmoreland." Her voice softened when she said his name.

And where was Joe Mack now? Divorced? Dead? And what about the absent Mr. Brown?

The need to know came unexpectedly to David, just as it had Sunday afternoon when Rosalie had stood in his yard with her home-baked apple pie.

With another man's name on her tongue, Rosalie stood looking at him, her eyes shining and her mouth soft and vulnerable. A quick pain stabbed at David's heart. In a moment of self-discovery he realized he was feeling envy.

Perhaps there was also hope.

"Well . . ." Rosalie said, looking at him expectantly. It must be his turn to say something, but all he could do right now was wonder at his envy for a man who was no longer around. "I'd better go in and change," she finally added. "I usually go for a walk when I get home, if the weather's pretty."

Her shoes crunched on the gravel as she walked away from him. The sun tipped its bowl of gold over her, setting her aglow so that the warmth of her squeezed his heart.

"Wait," he called, surprising both of them.

She glanced back over her shoulder, a dreamy look still on her face.

"We'll go with you, if you don't mind. Rover could use the exercise."

"I'll meet you here in a few minutes, then."

With a little wave of her hand, Rosalie left him. David watched her until she went inside her house. Was she as sweet, as trusting, as she seemed? What kind of woman didn't even hesitate when a man she knew nothing about suggested they walk together on streets that would soon be dark and empty?

And what kind of man asked? Here he was, deceiver of women, betrayer of love, reaching out for a woman he had no intention of inviting anywhere close to the vicinity of his heart. Gretchen had already labeled him a bastard, and now he labeled himself foolhardy as well.

"Selfish bastard," she had said. *"You murdered our marriage, you murdered our love. You destroyed everything we had."*

He guessed he could add lying to his list of sins and tell himself his motive for imposing on Rosalie's walk was need for exercise. He hadn't done much of it since leaving the police force. Two years ago he could have run across town and not been winded, but now he'd be lucky to run two miles before needing to rest.

Just because his heart would never be in shape again was no reason to neglect his body.

He smiled at Rosalie when she came to collect him for the walk. No need to inflict his dark secrets and black mood on her.

"Ready?" she asked.

"Ready."

They started down the street, side by side. David

let her set the pace. Rover bounded along in front of them, his tongue hanging out with joy.

"Am I going too fast?" she asked, her cheeks already turned rosy by the early October breeze.

"No."

"Too slow?"

"Just about right."

"Good. I mean . . . I'm not used to having a companion on these walks, so I don't know about keeping together."

"Neither do I." David adjusted to her pace. Keeping together. It felt good.

She cast him a sideways glance. Her eyes were especially beautiful with the late afternoon sun shining in them, the color of pansies and summer seas and moonlit skies all rolled into one. For the first time in many years, David longed to have an artist's brush in his hand.

"Why don't you know about keeping together, David?"

Her question took him by surprise. So did the fact that he wanted to give her an answer.

"I've been a loner for two years now."

"Divorced?"

"Yes." *Among other things.* "You?"

"Widowed. Twice."

So the absent Mr. Westmoreland and the absent Mr. Brown hadn't left her by choice.

"I'm sorry. It must have been very hard for you."

"Losing Joe Mack, my first husband, was like losing my heart, my soul. The boys were so young— only five. And I was hardly more than a child myself." She took a long breath, then turned to look directly into his eyes. "Losing Harry was a relief."

"If you want to tell me why, I'm a pretty good listener."

"Sometime . . . perhaps. But not today. I don't want to let bad memories spoil the walk."

Bad memories. Blood everywhere. Puddled in the alley. Squishing underneath his shoes. Covering his hands.

He wouldn't think about that right now. *Couldn't* think about that right now.

"David? Are you all right?"

Rosalie stopped and put her hand on his arm.

He looked at that small, fair hand with the brave red nail polish. Hard work had marked it. The knuckles were chapped, and the one on her empty ring finger was enlarged.

"David?" She patted his arm. "You made a sound . . . as if you were in pain."

He hadn't had anyone care about him in a very long time.

Memories washed over him once more, and with them came his twin enemies—guilt and rage. They jousted at his embattled spirit, and he gently removed Rosalie's hand from his arm.

"It must have been something in the air." He cleared his throat for emphasis.

Guilt smote him anew as Rosalie folded her hands tightly together. She was the last person in the world he wanted to hurt.

"Autumn allergies," she said. "Some people who have never had them develop allergies when they move to Tupelo. Perhaps we should go back."

"No . . . thank you. I don't want to spoil your walk."

"You didn't."

She smiled tentatively. He smiled hesitantly.

Dry leaves fluttered off the trees and rustled to the ground at their feet. A mockingbird high up in a chinaberry tree pretended to be a blue jay and crowed at them for tarrying. The sun, making its final lap toward its resting place, sent a rose-gold benediction over them.

A warmth that had nothing to do with the sun's rays stole over David. Like a weary traveler who finally catches his first glimpse of home, he drew a deep breath of relief. Reaching out, he clasped Rosalie's hand.

"Why don't we finish our walk?"

She glanced briefly at their entwined hands, and for a moment he thought she was going to pull away. Who could blame her if she did?

"Yes. Let's do. I'll tell you about the town."

With her small hand nestled in his, Rosalie described her town with pride and affection. The warm glow of an Indian summer evening combined with the musical lilt in Rosalie's voice lulled David into a sense of contentment. For a brief while he imagined that he was young and invincible and full of dreams. He imagined that happy endings could be forged with love and goodness and strength, and that evil could be kept at bay with a force of will.

Their walk came to an end before they were ready, and they found themselves standing in front of their houses. At the same time they glanced self-consciously at their joined hands, and simultaneously they let go.

"Thank you for the walk, Rosalie."

"Thank you for going with me." She looked up at him from under her lashes, not in the bold manner of worldly women but in the manner of a graceful, gracious woman who doesn't realize her own appeal. The look was so unexpectedly sensuous that David clenched his fists in his pockets to keep from reaching out and embracing her. "I walk almost every evening, if you'd like to join me."

"Thank you." It wasn't much of a reply, but he wasn't in much shape to reply. If he said yes, he would be playing with dynamite, and if he said no, he would be shutting the door on the first emotions he had felt in two years. He certainly had no intentions of getting involved with Rosalie, of using her for his own purposes, but it felt good to realize that he was, after all, human.

Rosalie smiled at him, gave that gay little wave he was becoming accustomed to, then turned and walked into her house.

She never lingered over good-byes, and that was just as well, for David hated long good-byes.

Rosalie was humming when she went inside her house. Humming felt so good that she put on a tape and began to sing along.

Across the way, the music drew David to his window. Her voice was clear and haunting, incredibly beautiful. And she was singing a love song. He knew the music well. "All I Ask of You" from *Phantom of the Opera*.

Stephanie had loved music. She used to play that tape over and over when they were on patrol together. Sometimes she even tried to sing. Her voice wasn't good, and they both knew it. They would laugh good-naturedly at the high notes missed and the notes sung flat.

One rainy night she had turned to him in the car after the last of the song had died away, her face earnest and open.

"Will you always take care of me, David?"

"Of course. That's what partners are for."

"Till death do us part?"

Till death do us part. The words from the past haunted him.

From the house next door Rosalie's voice soared like an angel, full of triumph and hope and—God help him!—a genuine emotion that sounded like love. He gripped the curtain, crushing it between his balled fists.

"Don't," he whispered. "Don't fall in love with me, Rosalie. I can't fall in love with you. I won't."

Her magnificent voice lifted and swelled in the shadows of his house. He closed his eyes. The music sliced into his heart as surely as knives had sliced into his back.

David groaned with the pain of love lost and love forbidden, and his agony had a name.

"Rosalie . . . Rosalie," he whispered, over and over.

For the rest of the week David studiously avoided being around when Rosalie came home for her evening walk. He set up his tools in his empty room, building his doghouses and birdhouses away from any view of the house next door. Away from temptation.

By Friday evening he was weary from fighting repressed emotion and edgy from denial. When he heard Rosalie's old car pull out for work, he knew what he was going to do.

With his mouth fixed in a grim line and his heart beating overtime, he set out for the Edge of Paradise.

When David stepped into the café, Rosalie almost dropped her pad and pencil. Excitement and confusion made her whole body flushed and hot. She was sure the customers would notice.

And David. What if he noticed? With a death grip on her pad and pencil, she tried to concentrate on what Mr. Hank Willie was saying.

"Make that three hot dogs instead of two,

Rosalie . . . and heavy on the pickle relish." Her customer, the owner of the local hardware store, was an old-timer, who had been coming to the café for as long as Rosalie could remember.

"You bet, Hank," she said, trying to keep her eyes off the table where David was sitting. It was impossible. He filled her vision, filled her senses. Their walk came back to her as clearly as the song she had sung Monday night—the way his hand had felt wrapped around hers, the sudden jolts of awareness when his shoulder accidentally brushed against hers, the feeling of togetherness that had lingered even after they'd parted.

"How are the boys?"

"Great. Lively as ever. Enjoying college." *David, David. Why have you been avoiding me? And why do I care?*

"The next time those devils are in town, you tell them Old Hank said hello."

"I will."

"And tell them for me that their mother is still pretty as a speckled pup."

"Thank you, Hank." David was looking her way. She turned her head so her hair hid her face from him. She didn't want him to see her flushed cheeks and get the wrong idea. Or any ideas at all.

Hank patted her hand. "Thank you, Rosalie, for brightening an old man's evenings for mighty nigh twenty years. No matter what kind of day I've had, I know I can always count on one of your smiles to cheer me up."

"It works both ways, Hank. *You* always cheer *me*." David was looking. She could tell by the crawly feeling at the back of her neck. *Please don't!* her mind screamed, even as her heart said *please do*.

Her hands trembled as she left Hank's table and

headed for the kitchen. She *did* want David Kelly to get ideas—and that was the whole trouble.

She placed Hank's order ticket on the carousel, and Betty looked at her as if she were a visitor from a foreign land.

"What's wrong, Rosalie?"

"Nothing." Rosalie pushed her hair back from her hot face.

"You look like you've been bargaining with the devil, honey. Are you sick?"

"No . . ." She glanced back over her shoulder. David had not let up his steady, unsettling study of her. "It's just that David Kelly is at table two."

"The neighbor you told me about last week?"

"Yes."

Betty leaned across the pass-through from the kitchen so she could get a better view. When she saw David, she pursed her lips in a silent whistle.

"You didn't tell me he was a dreamboat."

"It doesn't make any difference. Not one little bit." Rosalie retied her apron strings that didn't need retying.

"Rosalie . . . is something going on here?" Betty narrowed her eyes and put one stout fist on the counter, ready to do battle for her friend. "Has that man done something to you? If he has, you tell Big Betty, and I'll toss him out of here before he can say 'fried dill pickles.'"

"No!" Rosalie glanced over her shoulder in alarm, as if Betty had already socked David Kelly in the face. He was holding on to the menu but looking at her as if she might be his main course for dinner. She quickly turned back to Betty. "I'm just being silly, that's all. We went for a walk Monday night, and I haven't seen him since. . . ." She realized she was breathless. Pausing, she put her hand over her heart. It was racing as if she had run five miles.

"Are you sure you're all right?"

Rosalie managed a smile for her friend. "I guess this is called middle-age panic."

"Middle age, my Astroturf. Wait till you get fluffy and fifty." Betty glanced at table 2. "He's still watching you. Lord, his eyes look like two big old blue crystal balls or something. No wonder you're in a sexual sweat."

"Betty!" Rosalie leaned closer and whispered fiercely, "I'm not in a sexual sweat. I'm just not ready for this."

"Ready for what, honey?" Betty dropped the teasing and became the kindhearted confidante.

"I don't know . . . for feeling hot and cold all at the same time, for wanting to touch and be touched, for *hoping* . . ." Sighing, she paused and readjusted her apron. "I'd better get over to table two."

"Good luck, honey."

She was going to need it. Lord, when had she gone from curious but wary to almost smitten and scared? The closer she got, the more uncertain she became. David's eyes were fiercely alive, blazing with an unholy light, and yet his face was totally immobile, his expression neutral. Rosalie silently prayed for strength, but she didn't know whether she was praying for strength to resist him or strength to take a chance on him.

When she got close, she greeted him the way she did all her customers.

"Good evening." So far so good.

"Hello, Rosalie," he said, smiling, and she nearly fell apart.

He was magnificently masculine, wonderfully solid, and incredibly desirable. Her breath caught high in her throat, just from standing next to him in a crowded café. She didn't like to think of the state

she'd be in if they were in a secluded spot, surrounded by soft candlelight and romantic music.

Her hand tightened on her pencil. Everything she
should have said flew right out of her brain.

"How have you been this week, Rosalie?"

"Fine." *Lonesome.*

"I came to apologize for missing our walks together. I'm sorry, Rosalie."

"That's all right." *It had hurt.*

"No, it isn't." He caught her left hand, turned it
over, and studied the palm. "I should have called
and explained to you why I couldn't join you."

"I was home." *Waiting.*

"I know. I heard your car every evening." He smiled
at her, still holding her hand. "I guess I was listening
for it."

Did hearts take flight? Hers did. She could tell by
the rapid fluttering in her chest.

"I don't want to keep you from your work, but
there's more that I have to say."

"It's all right. I can take the time."

"I want you to know that I think you're a very fine
woman. I like you, Rosalie. I like you a lot."

"I like you, too, David."

"I'm glad."

He held her hand a while longer, tracing the
pattern of veins in her palm with his index finger.
She felt the heat of his touch all the way down to her
toes.

When she was certain that she'd melt into a
puddle at his feet, he released her hand.

"I'm a loner, Rosalie. I think I told you that. But I
do want us to be friends."

Friends? She breathed a sigh of relief mixed with
regret. "I'd like that, David."

"Good. That's settled, then." He smiled at her. "I'm
starved. What's the house specialty?"

"Meat loaf and fried green tomatoes."

"Sounds good to me. With lots of hot coffee."

Her step was jaunty as she walked back to the kitchen. Betty was waiting for her at the pass-through.

"Everything is okay, Betty. He wants to be friends. Don't look skeptical. He's a good man. I *know* he is."

"You don't have to convince me. I saw it all. The way he held your hand, the way he looked at you." She put her hands on her hips and tilted her head to one side. "Friends, huh?"

"That's what he said . . . and I said yes."

"Umm-hmm." Betty smiled and nodded, then got his order off the carousel. "Give me the biggest plate of loaf and fried tomatoes you got," she yelled toward the kitchen. "We got a hungry man out here."

Rosalie glanced at table 2. David was laughing.

Friends. She could handle that.

He loved watching her work. He lingered over his coffee, not even pretending to himself that it was time to go.

Rosalie moved through the small café with a grace that would have befitted a queen. It was obvious she took both joy and pride in her work. David liked that about her. Though he knew a little about her life, he didn't know exactly what circumstances had caused her to end up as a weekend waitress at a small café; but he was glad to see she had kept her grace and charm.

From time to time she glanced over her shoulder and smiled at him. He felt warmed by her smiles. In her rare free moments she came by his table with the coffeepot, making sure he always had a refill.

He guessed he'd had enough coffee in the last two

hours to supply troops at Camp Shelby. Still, he made no move to leave.

He watched as she came toward him.

"More coffee, David?"

He held his cup toward her, wanting to look rather than talk. When the cup was filled to the top once more, Rosalie lingered at his table. He tried to squash the selfish hope that sprang to life in him, but it refused to die.

"I guess you caught a taxi here," she said.

"No. I walked."

"That's a long walk."

He smiled. "Our workout Monday evening put me in shape."

He loved the way her eyes sparkled when he mentioned Monday. They had held hands. Judging by the shine in her eyes and his own racing pulse, he'd have thought they had shared a torrid evening in bed if he hadn't known better.

Whoa, boy. This is a friendship. Remember?

"It's not long till closing time." She waited; he watched. "You can ride home with me if you want to. . . ." She wet her bottom lip with her tongue. David squeezed the handle of the coffee cup. "If you're still here."

"I'll be here." He set the coffee cup on the table with great care, never taking his gaze from her. "I'd love to ride with you, Rosalie."

Four

I'd love to ride with you, Rosalie.

David's words echoed through her mind as they drove through the night streets together. He sat beside her, not too close but close enough that she could feel his pants legs barely brushing against her thigh. Glare from the streetlights highlighted the rugged planes of his face and the fierce gleam in his eye.

His words roared through her like cascading waters, and she clutched the steering wheel until her knuckles turned white. *Ride with you. Ride with you.*

A slow burn spread throughout her body. Her face felt flushed and hot.

Now *stop that*, she told herself. He hadn't meant a darned thing erotic or suggestive. He'd merely been talking about a ride in her car.

"Isn't that our street?"

"What?" She twisted to look at him.

"I thought you passed our street."

He was right. She had whizzed by her own street as if she'd never seen it before.

"Sometimes I come this way," she said, taking the

next left and going back a block. "For a change of scenery."

"That's a good idea. I sometimes like a change of scenery myself." She could have hugged him for not smirking. "I guess that's why I'm such a traveling man."

"Do you travel a lot, David?"

"Just in the last few years."

Their houses loomed large, two separate shadows waiting for them. In the glow of her dashboard lights they gazed at each other. Rosalie slowed the car to a crawl.

"You've been lots of exciting places, I guess," she said.

"Lots of places. None of them exciting . . . until I came here."

She let her foot completely off the accelerator, and the old car almost choked to a stop.

"Hmm," she murmured, letting him take it any way he wanted as she recovered and set the car back in motion.

"Have you always lived here, Rosalie?"

"Always. Once, when I was young, I dreamed of going to faraway places—New York, Paris, London." She was at the driveway now. "I was going to be a singer and perform in all the great opera houses. I learned a couple of languages in school, and Italian on my own. I was even studying with a good voice coach here in town. But the boys came when I was barely eighteen. Secretarial school was a practical choice." She shrugged her shoulders, smiling. "I wouldn't trade Jack and Jimmy for all the opera roles in the world."

She parked the car. It continued to shudder and cough after she turned off the key. David didn't seem to notice.

"And what about you, David? Tell me about your-self."

Instead of answering her, he reached for her face. "You sang Monday night," he said, his voice soft. Both hands on her cheeks, he slowly turned her to face him. "I thought I was hearing angels, Rosalie. I stood at the window listening to you. Your music touched my heart."

"Thank you." *I was singing for you, because of you.*

"And then—" he paused, caressing her chin with his thumbs—"you didn't sing anymore."

She felt as if she had left her ordinary body and her old car and was soaring in a sun-drenched meadow filled with fragrant flowers. She closed her eyes, letting the beauty wash over her.

"Was it because of me? Because I hurt you?"

"Oh, no." She put her hands on his face. "It was nothing you did. You could never hurt me."

"I'm glad. I don't want to hurt you, Rosalie." He gently traced her eyebrows, her cheeks, her lips. "I don't ever want to hurt you."

"You won't. . . ." He leaned close, so close. "You can't. . . ."

Rosalie didn't know who made the first move, but suddenly their lips brushed together, softly, gently, like the sigh of wind on waves, the kiss of dew on roses.

She almost stopped breathing. With his lips barely touching hers, they became suspended in time. She could feel the thud of his heart against the inside of her arm, hear the hurried rush of his breath against her skin.

Something beautiful was happening on this Indian summer night in the trembling darkness of a rickety old car. Both of them sensed it, felt it.

They held on to each other, unmoving, afraid to

lose the magic by letting go and afraid to claim it by reaching out. A lover's moon tracked across the sky, bathing them in a silvery glow.

Rosalie's lips trembled, and David responded.

"Don't be afraid." His mouth moved against hers as he formed the words.

"I'm not." Her words were only a sigh, a whispery breeze that carried her toward David.

Their lips met, and the kiss bloomed between them as if it were a beautiful bud awaiting the gentle rains and warm sunshine of their touch. Sighing, Rosalie laced her arms around David's neck, and he circled his around her waist.

All the music she'd wanted to sing pulsed through Rosalie, and all the beauty he'd wanted to paint washed over David. With their lips tenderly pressed together, they treated the kiss as something precious, not to be taken lightly and not to be taken for granted.

He didn't try to take more than she offered, and she didn't ask for more than he could give. Wonder trembled through them, and they held on, unwilling and unable to let go.

Finally, the time came, as they both knew it would, when the kiss had to end. They drew apart at the same time.

If they had been younger and less wise, they might have tried to deny what had happened, tried to pretend that it was merely a passing fancy, a meaningless impulse. But they both had known love, and they recognized its taste.

David cupped Rosalie's cheek with one hand. "I didn't mean to do that."

"Neither did I."

"It was beautiful, Rosalie. Special."

"I know."

His eyes darkened with guilt remembered, and

hers became bright with pain recalled. As they gazed at each other, the wonder that had sought to be born died a slow and merciless death.

"I don't want to give you false ideas," he said.

"And I don't mean to lead you on."

"I'm not ready for any of this . . . for the tender feelings, the need, the hunger." His hand tightened on her cheek. "I'm *hungry* for you, Rosalie. You're like a spring of fresh water that I've suddenly stumbled upon after years of wandering in the desert."

"I know . . . I understand." She leaned her cheek into his hand. "I guess we're both just lonely, David."

"Lonely as hell."

Summoning up courage she didn't feel, Rosalie smiled at him. "I don't want you to worry about this. I'm not some giddy teenager who's going to try to hold you to promises you never made. I'll just consider this a lovely end to a lovely evening."

"You're a wonderful woman, Rosalie—a beautiful, gentle, compassionate woman." He bent close and brushed his lips against her forehead. "I'm damned lucky to have you for a friend."

"And I'm thankful to have you." She straightened her shoulders and smiled with determination, breaking the somber mood. "Vacant houses always look so cheerless. Besides that, you have a dog. I'm crazy about dogs, but since the boys left, I haven't kept one because of my work. A dog would get too lonely staying home by himself all the time."

"You have a standing invitation to come and visit Rover any time you get lonesome."

He got out on his side of the car and came around to open her door. Taking her hand, he helped her out.

"Be careful what you promise," she said. "I may take you up on it."

He walked her to her door, then leaned down and kissed her cheek. "Good night, Rosalie."

She smiled, then gave him her special good-bye wave. She didn't look back as she walked through her door, but he stood in the driveway anyhow, watching as if he could still see her.

The moon vanished behind a cloud, and David stood in the darkness, waiting until Rosalie's light came on, signaling her safe arrival to her bedroom.

"Thanks for the ride," he whispered.

Then he went into his house for what he was absolutely certain would be one of his most tormented nights in a long, long time.

On Saturday morning David woke up to the sound of music. At first he thought it was the echo of Rosalie, singing through his heart. Then he realized it *was* Rosalie, singing in her kitchen.

She was singing an Italian aria. From *Madama Butterfly*, if he remembered correctly. Majestic and tender, the song brought tears to his eyes.

He turned his attention from the window and looked at his surroundings. Limp curtains, washed so many times they were drab and gray, hung at the windows. Faded roses stared back at him from the peeling wallpaper. The linoleum stretched across the floor, the color of old bologna, cracked and buckling so that he had to be always on his guard when he navigated across it.

His sanctuary. His prison.

For the first time in two years, he cared about his surroundings.

After his divorce, he had left Alabama with not much more than the clothes on his back, his art supplies, and his tools. Gretchen, contending she was the injured party, had taken everything in the divorce. He hadn't cared. When his lawyer became alarmed and went back to the negotiating table, she had generously offered him the dented stew pots and the toilet seats; but he had graciously declined.

He had sinned: He had to pay.

But now, with Rosalie's music sparkling in the air, he caught a glimpse of redemption, and with the redemption came the need to improve his surroundings.

He ate a quick breakfast of wheat flakes, entertained by a new aria drifting across the way, something lively. *The Barber of Seville* he thought.

Smiling, he found mop and mop bucket in the pantry and set to work. So intent was he on his chores that he didn't hear Rosalie until she was standing behind him.

"I knocked, but you didn't hear." She wore jeans and baggy sweatshirt that said HANG IN THERE BABY. Her shining hair was tied back in a red ribbon. She looked sixteen.

David felt seventeen.

"Hello there." He stood up, flexing knees that had gone stiff from squatting. "Housemaid's knees." He grinned at her.

"Rover let me in."

"The next thing I know, he'll be asking you to go dancing."

She tipped her head back when she laughed. The pale blue veins on the side of her neck gave David ideas—and they certainly weren't about scrubbing floors.

"I brought you something," she said.

"You shouldn't have . . . but I'm glad you did."

"It's not much. Just some quick-fix sticky buns I make with canned biscuits."

"Woman, you've lured me away from my mop."

His heart and soul cried out for a connection with

her, his arm around her shoulders, his hand upon her arm, his thigh brushing against hers. But what had happened the previous night had made him wary. Connections with Rosalie, even brief ones, were dangerous.

"Let's follow my nose," he said, leading the way back to the kitchen.

Her latest gift of food sat in the middle of his bare table, exuding the delicious aroma of butter and sugar and cinnamon. David poured two cups of coffee, and they sat across from each other, a bit self-conscious, a bit wary, sharing breakfast.

"I had an ulterior motive, you see."

"Don't tell me. Let me guess." David pretended to be deep in thought. Across the table Rosalie licked the icing on her right index finger. Desire shot through David so unexpectedly he almost lost his grip on his sticky bun.

"Well . . . I'm waiting." Her pink tongue flicked out once more to nip at the sugar icing.

The table that stood between them was both a hindrance and a help. If it hadn't been there, he might have lost all control. He might have licked her sugar icing without even asking if she wanted help.

As it was, the table provided a place to hide the almost painful state he was in.

"Still thinking?" she asked, taking one final, delicate lick at the sweets on her finger.

"Hmmm." He crammed his mouth full of food in order to give himself time to gain control. The sticky bun went down in one uncomfortable lump. He didn't know whether or not he chewed it.

"It seems to me you just used this food as a chance to come flirt with my dog," he was finally able to say.

"Exactly." Her happy laughter filled his kitchen, making it seem brighter, cleaner, *better*, than it was.

At the sound of his name Rover got up from his

nap in the corner and wandered over to lick Rosalie's ankles.

She laughed and patted his head while David watched with envy. When the dog had his quota of petting, he ambled back to his corner and settled in for what appeared to be hibernation rather than napping.

"You'll notice I selected the most vicious watchdog at the shelter."

"You should have named him Killer." Rosalie pushed her plate aside and stood up. "I'd better be going."

Her sudden decision caused a tumult of emotions in David, quick pain at losing her sweet presence followed by intense relief that he had been spared breaking his own rules.

"Busy day?" he asked, trying to seem just a friend.

"I'm going to negotiate a really clean deal with a pile of laundry, then I'm going to a clandestine appointment in a dark and shady pantry. There are some old cans of peaches getting uppity and a few sour pickles ready to revolt."

Almost recovered from the sugar-icing episode, David escorted her to the door.

"I'm glad you came over, Rosalie. Thanks for the food."

"Thank you, David, for the company." She squeezed his hand, and he tried not to take it personally. After all, he was the one who had made the rules. "I wasn't going to come here, but the recipe makes more than enough for one." Her pink tongue flicked over her lips, as if sugar still lingered there. He guessed that it did, Rosalie's own special brand of natural sweetness. The remembered taste still lingered in his mind.

"Anyhow," she added as she fiddled with the ribbon that bound her hair, "we both agreed to be friends, and I knew you wouldn't misinterpret my visit."

"Sharing a meal is far more pleasant than eating alone."

With a wave she was gone, back across her yard and into her house. David cursed the fates that made rules necessary with Rosalie, then took up his cleaning supplies and scrubbed his house with a vengeance.

They both spent the rest of the day studiously avoiding their windows and congratulating themselves on their discipline and their sensible decision to keep a safe distance.

Just friendship. They could handle that.

David tried not to notice when Rosalie's car pulled out that evening. He tried not to think of her in the café, smiling at other people. Would she look for him at table 2? Would she miss him if he didn't come?

"Dammit." He threw his dishes into the sink with unnecessary force. Rover wandered over and sniffed his legs, then meandered back to his dog dish.

David thought of Rover licking Rosalie's legs. "Dammit," he said again.

He soaped his dishes twice, scrubbing them with the same vigor he had used on his house.

"Repressed sexual urges. It's a hell of an incentive to clean the house, Rover."

Filled with restless energy, David roamed his house after he finished the dishes. Rover trailed along behind him. He picked up and rejected all his books. He considered, then vetoed, every movie listed in the newspaper. What he needed was a task that would consume him.

When the solution came to him, it was more than an answer; it was a revelation, a compulsion, a passion. Hurrying, he went into his bedroom and took his art supplies from their storage place.

He held a sable brush in his hand, glorying in the feel. It had been so long.

A secret hopeful place in his heart had been touched, and now it was awake to dreams of color and form and beauty, dreams he had thought were dead.

David took out his sketch pad and carried it to the rickety desk in his den. The light was bad. He'd have to get some lamps.

His hands felt clumsy at first, uncertain, but soon they took up the rhythms they knew so well. Time melted and flowed by. A face emerged on the pad.

Rosalie.

He traced the sketch with his fingers. *Rosalie*, down at the café in an old car that might never make it back home.

David pitched his pad on the desk and glanced at his watch. Ten o'clock. The café closed at eleven. He could make it.

When he reached the café, he saw her through the green-tinted windows. She was bending over a table in the subtly provocative way that was sexier because it was totally unconscious.

His pulse raced, and his heart throbbed. Whom was he trying to kid? He hadn't come to the café to protect her from an old car that might go dead on dark, deserted streets. He hadn't come for coffee. He had come to watch, to long, to hope.

He had come to prove how strong he was, how dependable, how trustworthy. He turned to leave, but she saw him.

Astonishment, then joy, lit her face, and she lifted her hand in greeting.

David went inside. He would order coffee and escort her home. Nothing more.

Five

The rains had started before they left the café. By closing time, a storm was brewing. Great slashes of lightning lit the sky, and loud crashes of thunder echoed through the almost-empty city streets.

"And I didn't even bring an umbrella," Rosalie said, standing in the doorway of the café looking out.

"Neither did I. I didn't expect rain." David whisked off his coat. "Maybe this will help."

"You'll freeze."

"I'll survive." He held the coat over her head with one hand and pulled her close with the other. Electrical currents pulsed through them, but not from the storm. Both of them pretended not to notice. "Hold tight, Rosalie."

They ran through the rain, pressed together like bookends to a book, hip against hip, thigh against thigh, shoulder against shoulder. The storm beat at them with a fury that was almost malicious.

By the time they reached Rosalie's car, they were soaked.

"You drive," she said.

The storm had driven away the last vestiges of

Indian summer, and the car was cold inside, cold and damp with the increased humidity.

"You're shivering." David cranked the car, then put his arm around Rosalie's shoulders, pulling her close. "You'll be warmer over here. Body heat."

Rosalie didn't protest. His arm around her felt too good.

Body heat. If only he knew. She felt the searing heat of him all the way to her bones. It melted her. She felt liquid and languorous. She had to exert great effort to keep her head from lolling on his shoulder.

"Comfortable?" he asked.

"Hmmm." *Heavenly.*

"Great. Let's head for home."

It sounded so good when he said it. *Home.* As if it were a place they shared, a place with two chairs by the fire and matching mugs for hot coffee and two dented pillows on a bed with a feather comforter.

Except that she didn't need the feather comforter. Not with the amount of body heat David was putting out.

David drove through the streets without speaking. But he kept one arm wrapped tightly around Rosalie.

She imagined how it would be if he were always there waiting for her.

They would laugh together as they had over the sticky buns. They'd share music; he had said he loved it. They would cuddle by the fire, or perhaps dance, holding each other so close, she couldn't tell where she ended and he began.

Fantasizing again. She was going to have to stop it.

Thunder rattled the car windows, and rain collected in small rivers.

"Looks like the streets are going to flood," David said.

"Sometimes it happens . . . with this much rain."

Rosalie couldn't get worked up about a flood on the streets. She was too busy trying to stay sane.

The heat building in her was now a full-fledged conflagration. Her body felt limp; her legs felt wobbly. She didn't know how she would manage to get into her house.

Great sheets of water were spewing up from the tires by the time they reached Rosalie's street. David slowed the car to a crawl so it wouldn't hydroplane through the water.

Rosalie wished the ride could go on forever.

"I'll see you to your door," he said as he parked the car.

"There's no need. You'll get soaked."

"I already am."

They ran through the rain once more, clinging together under David's wet coat. At her door, Rosalie fumbled with her key.

"Wet hands," she said.

"Let me help you." David steadied the key by putting his hand over hers. He stood close behind her, pressing his chest into her back. Rosalie shivered. "You're freezing. Do you have a fireplace?"

"Yes."

"I'll come in and build a fire."

You already have.

He followed her inside, and suddenly her drab little rental house seemed beautiful. With his warmth and strength and vitality filling the rooms, they took on a charm they had never had.

Rosalie stood with her arms wrapped around herself, watching David build the fire. He got dry logs from the back porch, stacked them inside the fire-place, lined the kindling underneath.

She knew there were things a good hostess would be doing—fetching towels to dry their hair, brewing hot coffee, fluffing pillows.

Now there was a thought. Pillows side by side on the bed. David's head denting one, hers the other.

He found the matches without her help, in a small box atop the mantel. The tiny flame flared, then caught. Burning wood crackled in the stillness.

David stood up, then turned to her. His wet shirt hugged a very broad chest, and the wet jeans clung to his muscular thighs. Rosalie hadn't seen that much man so close up in fourteen years. She shivered.

"You're still freezing." David wrapped his arms around her and brought her close to the fire. She leaned into him, loving the way her wet body felt against his.

"Stay right here," he said. "Don't move."

She couldn't have moved if wild elephants had been stampeding toward her. Weak-kneed, she watched as David started down her hallway. He made a turn into her bedroom, backed up, then went across the hall into her bathroom.

When he came back, he was carrying two pink towels. Without a word he began to dry her hair. One by one he lifted damp strands of her hair and rubbed them between dry towels. Rosalie hadn't felt so cherished since Joe Mack had died.

She closed her eyes. Everywhere his hands touched her scalp, she felt a tingle. His touch was warm, tender, and exceptionally erotic. Closing her eyes, she leaned into him.

She sensed rather than felt the towels fall away. David's hands were in her hair, his fingers spread over her scalp, massaging gently.

Heat from the fire toasted her cheeks, but it was heat from David that burned her body. She didn't know who made the first move, but suddenly they were in each other's arms, wet and wild and hungry.

There was no gentle kissing this time, no delicate joining of lips. His mouth was demanding, hers wanton. They tasted each other until tasting was not enough. The tip of his tongue seared across her lips. She opened for him, and he plunged inside. Groaning, he explored her mouth, expertly, thoroughly.

She took his tongue deep inside, toying with it, sucking it. Sanity fled. David cupped her hips and fitted her tightly against his groin.

A rhythm as old as time overtook her. She swayed against him, gently at first, and then with increasing fervor.

"Rosalie . . . Rosalie." His lips left hers and seared down the side of her neck.

"Please . . ." She rocked against him, feeling his wet jeans grind into her skirt and wanting more, ever so much more.

One hand left her hips and found the buttons on her blouse. In a fog of passion she felt his hands upon her breasts, hot and possessive.

"You are beautiful . . . exquisite."

She didn't want to be admired; she wanted to be possessed. Instinctively, she pulled his head down to her breasts. His warm breath fanned against her skin as he bathed her nipples with his tongue.

She clung to him, mindless now. The part of herself she had kept deeply buried was suddenly alive, alive and demanding attention. Fear vanished. Caution fell by the wayside.

She tugged at his shirt, pulling it loose from his waistband. Her hands inched underneath, touching his skin, tentatively at first, and then with boldness and joy.

For Rosalie there was only the moment—the fire inside and the storm without—and David, who had found the magic. She whispered his name, over and over, and the sound was like music.

"David . . . David. Please."

Her hands climbed upward under his shirt, warm against his skin, gentle. He was free-falling, plunging downward at breakneck speed with no way to stop.

She whispered to him, moving her hands over his skin in ways both tender and erotic. He wanted her. She wanted him. They were both free. It all seemed so simple.

They swayed together, tasting, touching, feeling. And then her hand flattened over his scar. She went very still.

"David?" she whispered, leaving the question unspoken.

How could he have forgotten? he wondered. How could he have been so careless?

"It's nothing, Rosalie," he whispered. "Nothing."

Satisfied, she moved against him once more, murmuring sweet words of encouragement.

He had lied. The scar couldn't be dismissed as *nothing*. It was his judge, his jury, his sentence.

He had to let Rosalie go.

He eased back a little, separating himself from the tantalizing motion of her hips. The pain of denial was so great, he groaned. Her skin was warm under his mouth, warm and fragrant and inviting. One more taste. That was all he needed.

He took her nipple deep into his mouth, savoring that one last forbidden taste while damning himself for being a selfish bastard. He couldn't let go abruptly. He couldn't just back off. Both of them were too close to the edge.

He gentled her with his hands, his mouth, easing

them away from the dangerous precipice that yawned before them. His hands moved up and down her back in long, gentle strokes. He brushed tender kisses across the tops of her breasts, up the side of her neck, until he found her lips once more.

She opened her mouth for him, teasing with her tongue, inviting him in, but he steadfastly refused the invitation. With a control he was far from feeling, he tried to bring them back to the beginning of their friendship, when their kisses had been simple and sweet.

Rosalie stiffened. "David?" she murmured, her lips still against his.

"I'm sorry, Rosalie."

"You're sorry?" She leaned back in his arms, staring at his face.

"I didn't mean to let it go that far." He pulled her blouse onto her shoulders and began to fasten the buttons. She pushed his hand away.

"I wanted it to, David." With great dignity Rosalie stepped out of his embrace and arranged her clothes. Her cheeks were rosy with embarrassment, and her eyes were bright and damp. "I guess I still do."

He had made her cry. The knife that sliced at his heart was just as real as the one that had sliced his back. He swore silently, damning himself to the deepest pits of hell. One or two violent words must have escaped, for suddenly Rosalie was beside him, her hand resting tenderly upon his face.

"David . . . don't. I led you on."

"Led me on?"

"Like a wanton woman. You're strong and tender, virile and appealing."

One tear trembled on her lash, then trailed silently down her cheek. David didn't dare brush it away.

"And I . . ." Rosalie paused, wetting her lips.

Desire, fierce and threatening, washed through David, almost overwhelming him. "It's been so long, David. What Joe Mack and I had was wonderful, tender, precious, and extremely satisfying . . . even though we were just kids."

She released his hand and stepped back. "I guess you remind me of him, a little. You've unearthed that part of myself I've kept buried."

Every bit of the pain he felt was reflected in her face. Their eyes held for a heart-wrenching moment, and then she looked away.

"I'm sorry, David," she whispered.

"Dammitall to hell." He gripped her shoulders, forcing her to look at him. "You have nothing to be sorry about. Do you understand?" Her eyes widened as she stared at him, and he saw her fear. It was only a fleeting emotion, but he recognized it.

He released her and strode across the room, swearing in earnest now. What kind of monster had he become?

"I wanted you." He turned back to her, moderating his voice. "I still do. It's that simple. Every time I get near you, every time I touch you, I want you so much, it's a physical pain."

She sucked in her breath. He saw hope come into her eyes.

"None of this is your fault, Rosalie. I'm to blame. I lost control." The light in her eyes almost blinded him, almost swayed him from his course. "It won't happen again. I promise you that."

Rosalie moved across the room, her wet clothes clinging to her body with an intimacy he envied. She sat in a comfortable-looking plaid chair and folded her hands in her lap.

"No. It won't happen again, David. It was my mistake as much as yours."

There was so much he wanted to say, so much he

wanted to do. But it would only prolong the agony, postpone the inevitable.

The fire crackled in the still room, and the storm moaned around the windows.

I can't love you, Rosalie. Don't ask me to. The words he couldn't speak echoed through his heart.

He lingered, savoring one last precious glance of the gentle woman who had come unexpectedly into his life.

"Don't stop singing because of tonight, Rosalie."

She smiled wistfully and pushed her damp hair away from her flushed face. David knew that she wouldn't be the one to say good-bye.

Neither could he.

He lifted his hand in salute, then headed for the door, leaving behind a cheerful room and a warm and lovely woman. Parting was a small death.

Rosalie sat in her chair, afraid to move. She thought she might break into a thousand pieces if she did.

Tears coursed down her cheeks; cold dampness seeped into her body. She would be warm if she moved closer to the fire, but she didn't figure her legs worked yet. Her whole body was still limp with desire.

What a fool she'd been. Throwing herself at David like a love-starved widow. She guessed that's what she was. That, plus more. She was uneducated, ordinary, as unexciting as the old gray paint peeling off the side of her house.

A man like David Kelly was bound to want more. She'd bet his wife had had at least one degree. She might even have been the kind who could juggle marriage with an exciting career and make them both work. David deserved that kind of woman.

Oh, she had been so foolish.

Rosalie got up from her chair and poked the fire David had built. Sparks shot up from the poker, and the wood crackled. It sounded so friendly, so cheerful. Any woman in her right mind would have responded.

She guessed she wasn't in her right mind.

Rosalie wandered over to her window and looked across the way. Every light in David's house was on. He was prowling from room to room like a caged panther.

"Serves you right. You could have been in my bed."

Still burdened with the awful knowledge that she had somehow failed, Rosalie turned from her window. Her clothes were beginning to dry. She was warming up, thawing out. And with the thawing came anger. Not at David, but at herself.

What had happened merely repeated an old pattern of hers: She was *accommodating*. True, she had wanted David as much as he had seemed to want her, but the fact was, she had been willing to make love to a man she knew nothing about. She had been willing to *settle*.

"Rosalie Tompkins Westmoreland Brown," she whispered softly as she squatted in front of the fire. "Perennial caretaker."

She had adored Joe Mack Westmoreland, loved him with all the intensity of her seventeen-year-old heart. But she hadn't wanted to marry him—not for a few years at least. She had planned to go to college and study music, then have a career in opera. And then she had got pregnant.

Her dreams of an opera career and his of an engineering degree were replaced by the practicalities of day-to-day living. She had settled for secretarial school, and Joe Mack had settled for garage mechanic.

And then there was Harry. She was lonely; he was kind, or so she had thought. When the marriage went bad, she had wanted out, but he had begged her to stay. And so she had settled again, trying to make it work.

Rosalie stood up and viciously stoked the fire with the poker. Never again. She was through with settling.

Not that David Kelly was the kind of man one settled for. He looked like the grand prize to her. But then, she didn't know a thing about him.

She turned her head toward his house and saw him silhouetted through the window. His chest was bare, and his jeans were molded to his hips and thighs. He looked like one of those cardboard posters for fitness centers, the kind that came with the admonishment "In six weeks you can look like this."

Rosalie sighed. He had been a nice fantasy.

The following day she was going to turn over a new leaf, become a new woman, begin a new life. She had had dreams once. It was time to dust them off and take a good look at them. It was time to see if she could make any of them come true.

David had planned to leave without saying good-bye.

In the early Sunday-morning hours, long before the lights were on in Rosalie's house, he stood in his bedroom with his bags packed. He would forfeit the rest of his rent. It was a small price to pay for freedom.

Freedom. Is that what he had, running from town to town, trying to escape his memories?

He sank onto the edge of his bed. Rover padded over to him and licked his hand. *Damn.* He had already formed a tie in this town. The dog. He couldn't just leave without making arrangements for his dog. And he certainly couldn't take Rover with him. He might end up next in a place with no pets allowed.

He knew only two people in town: Rosalie and the pet-shop owner. The shop wouldn't take in an unpedigreed mutt, and he definitely couldn't ask Rosalie to take care of his dog.

He had already asked too much of her.

Rosalie. Even thinking her name was painful.

"Selfish bastard."

Rover flattened his ears and tipped his head to look up at his master.

"It's all right, boy. I wasn't talking about you." He patted the small dog's head.

Would Rosalie feel rejected when she awakened? Discarded? Angry? She had every right to be.

Across the way he saw her lights come on. Soon she would be in her kitchen, climbing on a stool to reach her cereal.

He owed her an explanation. Anything less would be cowardly.

Rosalie lost her breath when she saw David standing outside her door. Her first instinct was to welcome him with a smile as if nothing had happened. Her second was to run to her bedroom, climb into bed, and pretend she was asleep and couldn't hear him knocking. Her final decision, the one she considered wise and mature and in keeping with her resolution to be a new woman, was to let him in but treat him with proper caution.

She climbed off her stool, fastened the top buttons on her robe, and went to the door.

"Rosalie, I need to talk to you. May I come in?"

He had dark circles under his eyes, and he had

nicked himself shaving. Sympathy rose in her, but she fought it off. She was finished being a caretaker.

"Come in." She held the door wide, then stood back so no part of David's big body would brush against hers when he came inside.

They faced each other, and an awkward silence stretched between them. David was the one who broke it.

"Do you mind if we sit down?"

"I'll get some coffee." It gave her something to do. Her hand shook only a little when she handed him the cup.

"Thanks. I didn't sleep much last night."

"Neither did I."

"That's why I came, Rosalie. About last night."

"It's over and done with. We both agreed." She took a small sip of her coffee, watching him over the rim of her cup. "I'm adult enough to accept that."

"You're a sweet woman. A wonderful woman."

So wonderful you walked out the door. She gripped her cup with both hands, afraid to trust herself to say anything.

"My leaving last night had nothing to do with you. I want you to know that."

Was that supposed to be a consolation prize? Was it supposed to make her feel better? Oh, she was in a foul mood today. Playing the rejected lover to the hilt.

Well, why not? Why not leave somebody else to flounder for a while?

She sat with her coffee cup, leaving the burden of conversation on him and not really liking the new Rosalie she had become.

David's hands were steady on his coffee cup. His expression told her nothing. It was his eyes that seared her soul.

"I am . . . was a cop, Rosalie."

"I thought you were a carpenter."

"Only in the last two years . . . since I left Red Bay. I'm good with my hands."

I'll say! A trickle of sweat inched between her breasts. She remembered David's hands upon them, his mouth.

She sat stiffly in her chair, holding on to her coffee cup and praying. *Lord, let me get through the next few minutes without making a fool of myself.*

"My marriage . . . I told you I was married."

"Yes."

"What I didn't tell you was that it was a bad marriage, right from the start. Both of us were to blame. We didn't have the same goals, the same needs, the same . . . anything."

"And so you divorced?"

"No. We stayed together, trying to make it work."

Like Harry and me, she thought. But she didn't say anything. This was David's story, not hers.

"There is nothing lonelier than two people living in the same house without love. Our lives became as bleak as our marriage." David pushed his cup aside and raked his hands through his hair. "I finally couldn't endure it anymore. I asked Gretchen for a divorce, but she begged me to stay."

Her coffee had gone cold. Unwilling to leave David's side, Rosalie drank it that way.

"I stayed, Rosalie, even though I knew it was a mistake, even though I knew it was wrong."

"So did I. With Harry. Does that make us noble, or does it make us fools?"

"It made me a liar and a cheat, Rosalie. I fell in love with my partner, Stephanie. I think I knew it a long time before I finally admitted it." He stood up and began to pace, as if his memories were too powerful to allow him any peace.

"The department had rules about that sort of

thing. I broke all the rules." **His back was** to her, stiff with tension. Suddenly, he **strode** to her chair, leaned down to her, and **gripped her** shoulders. "Do you understand what I'm saying?"

"Yes."

"I cheated . . . once. I swore never to do it again. So did Stephanie. We both knew it was wrong."

David's hands bit into her shoulders. She welcomed the pain.

"And you love her still, David?"

He stepped back, his face and body as rigid as if he had been carved from a mighty oak. For a moment she thought he was going to walk out again, without another word.

And then he spoke.

"I loved her so much, I killed her."

Six

"No! You couldn't have."

"I did."

Rosalie stood up, clutching her gown close around her throat, all color drained from her face.

"You murdered her?" she whispered.

David had been so caught up in the past that he was almost totally oblivious to his present. Seeing Rosalie's face, the fear that came into her eyes, he felt like a monster.

"I didn't murder her. Not in the way you're thinking." Some of her color came back, but she still stood clutching her robe.

"We were on assignment. The kids were in a dark alley, full of drugs and looking for trouble. Our love had made us careless. We didn't know they had knives until it was too late."

"The scar on your back? Is that how you got it?"

"Yes." David went to her and put his hands on her shoulders. "I'm sorry, Rosalie. I didn't mean to frighten you."

"You didn't." She licked her dry lips, then sat down. "Actually, David, you did. Not that I thought

you were capable of such a thing . . . but I sometimes don't trust my own judgment . . . since
Harry."

David squatted beside her chair and took her
hands. They were cold. All thoughts of his own past
vanished.

"What did he do to you?" She looked at him with
eyes gone bleak. He chafed her hands gently between his. "Can you tell me, Rosalie? Can you talk
about it?"

For a moment she stared at him, as if deciding
whether to trust him. Then she sighed softly and
began to talk. She told the whole story—how Harry
had won her, wooing her at the café with sweet
promises and kind words, how his kindness had
gradually turned to cruelty, how she had wanted out
and he had begged her to stay, and how, finally, his
cancer had forced her to stay and take care of him.

When she had finished, he held out his arms, and
she came to him. They clung together, with David
squatting beside her chair and Rosalie leaning into
him. And if he had been asked, he couldn't have told
who was giving and who was receiving. It was one of
those rare and beautiful moments when two souls
touched, when two people recognized their separate
tortures and came together to comfort and protect
each other.

"I'm sorry, Rosalie," he whispered.

"I'm sorry, too, David."

She leaned her head on his shoulder, sighing. A
gentleness stole over David's spirit, and he almost
believed in dreams once more. He put his hand in
her hair, touching the silky strands with a posses-
siveness that astonished him.

Was this love? he wondered. This tender invasion
of the heart?

From the wall in Rosalie's kitchen came the chime of a clock. It was time to go.

David leaned back to look into her face. "Will you be all right, Rosalie?"

"Yes." She gave him a brave smile. "I'm determined to be."

He let her go, and they both stood up, acutely conscious of the intimacy they had just shared. He squeezed her hand lightly, and then let go.

"Take care of yourself, Rosalie."

"You, too, David."

It was their way of saying good-bye. He left her standing there, then turned at the kitchen door. She lifted her hand in the eloquent gesture he knew so well. A quick, sharp pain of regret squeezed his heart, and he almost turned back.

Leaving was the noblest course of action. She had been hurt enough. He turned away from her, closing the door without a sound.

"Rosalie, are you going to play that king you keep waving around in the air, or are you going to marry it?" Betty narrowed her eyes, studying her friend. She had come to Rosalie's for a game of gin rummy, as she sometimes did on Monday night.

"Sorry." Rosalie put her king in the discard pile. "Lost my concentration."

"You never had it." Betty plunked her cards on the table, then got up and poured herself another cup of coffee. "Want some?"

"No. Caffeine at night makes me jittery."

She left her chair and prowled around her kitchen, moving the coffee canister from one cabinet to the other, lining up the sugar canister with the flour, straightening the dish towels. She ended up at the window.

"That's the fifth time," Betty said.

"For what?"

"Lining up the canisters. You're going to wear holes in them." Betty got a handful of cookies from the cookie jar, then sat down at the table with her bounty. "If you want to go over there and stare out the window, why don't you just do it—instead of pretending you just got over there by accident?"

"Oh." Caught, Rosalie whirled around, her cheeks turning pink.

"You want to tell me what's going on between you and David?"

"It's nothing."

Betty snorted. "Is that how come you were at the café last night looking like death, and he didn't show up at all, after he'd been sitting at table two all weekend."

"You noticed?"

"Yeah. I noticed. But I tried to keep my mouth shut." Betty took a big bite of cookie, studying Rosalie as she chewed. "I figured if you needed a friend, you'd come to me."

Rosalie left the window and covered Betty's hand with hers. "You *are* a friend. And if I need to talk, I'll come to you."

"Thanks." Betty blinked to hide the moisture that came into her eyes, and Rosalie swallowed a sudden lump in her throat. "Well, are we going to play gin rummy, or are we both going to tune up and cry?"

"Let's play the game."

They played the game, and after Betty left, Rosalie wandered back to her window. David was sitting in his den, holding on to a book but staring at the wall.

Loneliness climbed into Rosalie's chest and took up residence there. Gripping the curtain, she watched him. When she finally let go of the fabric, it was crushed and wrinkled.

Rosalie smoothed the curtain, then straightened her shoulders and went into her bedroom. After she put on her gown, she climbed between her covers and pulled them up to her chin.

She didn't even glance at the empty pillow on the other side of her bed.

Nobody wanted a stray mutt.

David had tried for three days to find a home for Rover. Randy Prescott at the pet shop knew of no one who would take him in.

"You might inquire up at city hall," he said as he paid David for the latest birdhouses. "There's always lots of people coming and going up there. Somebody might want him."

"Thanks."

David left without mentioning that he would be leaving town as soon as he found a home for his dog. No use advertising his plans until they were complete.

He walked west toward the heart of the city. The air had a wintry bite in it, and he pulled his collar up against the chill. Winter would be coming soon. It was not a good time to move, especially since he didn't have a car. He needed to be settled into a new place before the cold weather came in earnest.

Maybe he should head farther south.

On his way down Broadway toward city hall he passed the Lyric Theater. There were no glitzy posters advertising the latest Hollywood offering, for the old building had long since been abandoned as a movie house and turned into a community playhouse. Rosalie had spoken with a certain longing when she'd told him of the theater.

He glanced at the marquee. *Oliver!*, it said. December 15, 16, 17. Tryouts were slated for Sunday afternoon.

David's quest for a new owner for Rover was forgotten. Rosalie had been planning to sing at the great opera houses of the world. "*Dreams rarely come true,*" he had told her.

He stood with his hands in his pockets staring at the marquee. He remembered *Oliver!* He had seen it once when he and Gretchen were at a police convention in Birmingham, Alabama. It was a musical, with a very good part for a female singer, if he remembered correctly.

Dreams rarely come true.

He was going to change that. For Rosalie. Giving her a dream would cost him nothing except a few more days in Tupelo—and a few more days of secretly gazing out his window.

Rosalie was checking the ads for voice coaches when the doorbell rang. Wednesday night. She wasn't expecting anyone.

The bell rang again. She underlined the name that sounded most promising, then went to her door. David was there with a single pink rose in one hand and a piece of paper in the other.

"David?"

"This is not about you and me, Rosalie."

She stood clinging to the doorframe, fighting the unreasonable surge of joy she felt.

"Then what is it about?"

"You have every right to be angry. I betrayed your friendship."

"We both did." She held the door open. "Come in out of the cold."

He stood just inside the door. She moved to the

other side of her kitchen table and hung on to the back of a chair. It helped, but not much.

"This is for you."

David held the rose toward her. Cautiously, she came around her chair and took it, being careful not to brush her hand against his.

Their gazes locked for a moment, and she felt herself falling victim to her passion. As if he had read her thoughts, David reached out and cupped her cheeks.

"You have nothing to worry about, Rosalie. I promise that I won't let things get out of hand."

"Speak for yourself, David."

A light leaped in the center of his eyes and then was gone. Rosalie pulled out of his reach. The journey to her cabinets for a bud vase was endless, a scorching, exhausting journey across the Sahara. Her throat felt parched. She felt weak and lethargic.

Oh David, David. I want you.

As she filled the bud vase, she let the rush of cool water run over her hands. She borrowed time by dawdling over the arrangement of the pink rose. The silence in her kitchen crashed around her, and David's still presence screamed through her mind.

Finally, she turned back to him. "Thank you for the rose. I love pink."

"I know." He smiled. "Because of your pink gown and robe."

A flush of heat threatened to swamp her. She set the bud vase in the middle of her table, then sank into a chair.

"Won't you sit down?" she asked, belatedly remembering her manners.

"I won't take that much time." He left the doorway and moved to the other side of her table. "I wanted you to have this, Rosalie."

He spread out a flyer, announcing Tupelo Community Theater's production of *Oliver!* Leaning forward, she traced her hands over the letters.

"I thought of you when I saw this."

I needed nothing to make me think of you.

"I thought of you singing in your kitchen. You have a beautiful voice, Rosalie."

"Not good enough for the stage."

"How do you know?"

"It's rusty with disuse. It's untrained."

"This is not professional theater; it's community theater."

"Are you suggesting I try out for a role?"

"That's exactly what I'm suggesting."

"Why?"

Why indeed? David wondered. His reasons were so complex, even he couldn't comprehend them. He settled for telling her as much as he knew to be the truth.

"I want to do something to make up for the way I treated you."

"You didn't . . ."

He held up his hand, interrupting her. "Hear me out, please." He pulled out a chair and straddled it, then leaned across the table toward her. "I'm leaving, Rosalie."

"No . . ."

"As soon as I can find a home for my dog. But before I go, I want to give you a dream . . . at least, a part of a dream. I told you once that dreams rarely come true. I've changed my mind about that, Rosalie. At least where you're concerned."

Her hand trembled on the poster, and his inched across the table. Their fingertips brushed together, lightly. Currents arced between them, hot, fiery currents that couldn't be denied. They laced fingers, then locked hands, palm to palm.

He searched her face, and she searched his. Both

of them saw desire and need and hope, struggling to be reborn.

"Don't leave because of me," she whispered. "I couldn't bear it if you left because of me."

"It's because of me. It's time to move on." His hand tightened on hers, then let go.

"Where will you go?"

"Probably south, toward Florida."

"And then . . . ?"

"I don't know."

She caressed the poster as if it were a lover. David was giving her a dream.

"Stay," she said suddenly.

"I can't."

"Can't or won't?"

He was silent, watching her with a quiet regard that set her blood racing. Rosalie picked up the poster, folded it, and put it in her pocket.

"I'll try out for this musical on one condition."

"Name it."

"If I get the role, you'll stay long enough to see me perform."

"That's blackmail, Rosalie."

"Call it what you like. Those are my conditions."

"And if I say no?"

She stood up, planted her hands on the table, and leaned so close, she was nose-to-nose with him.

"Then you can take your dream and go straight to hell."

The shock of hearing her cuss made him speechless. Watching his face, Rosalie held her breath. Being a brave new person was harder than she had thought.

Suddenly, David laughed. It was a big, booming sound that filled her kitchen. Rosalie joined in.

After the laughter had died down, David stood up, facing her.

"You know, the thing that fascinates me most about you, Rosalie, is that you keep surprising me."

"Lately, I've been surprising myself."

"Good luck with the role."

"Does that mean you're staying?"

"Long enough to see you front and center on that stage."

Sweet relief flooded her. She wanted to throw her arms around him and hold on tight. Instead, she held out her hand.

"It's a deal."

When David got home, he unpacked his bags. He'd been living out of them since Sunday night.

His step was jaunty as he replaced his belongings on the shelves. When he unpacked his art supplies, he stood very still.

Across the way he heard music. "As Long As He Needs Me," from *Oliver!* Rosalie was practicing.

David set up his easel. He was whistling.

Mr. Mackey was the first to notice the change in Rosalie. He was the senior law partner at the firm where she worked, and the one she liked best.

"Are those roses I see in your cheeks, young lady?"

"Could be. I'm going to try out for a singing role in the community theater."

"I didn't know you sang."

"I haven't much, until lately."

"I approve. A person should always try new and different things. If you need time off from work for rehearsals, let me know."

"I haven't got the part yet."

"You will."

Friday night Betty told her the same thing. "Listen,

honey. It will be a pure privilege to have a celebrity working around here."

"But if I get the part . . ."

"You will."

". . . I can't take time off with pay."

"I don't want to hear any argument about it. I'm running this place, and I do it like I damned well please . . . and don't you give me any sass about it."

"Yes, ma'am." Rosalie gave a smart salute, then hugged Betty's neck.

The pink rose David had brought her gradually drooped and withered, but Rosalie couldn't bring herself to throw it away. On Sunday afternoon before the tryouts, she gently took the rose from its vase, wiped the water from the stem with a paper towel, then laid it in the sunshine on her windowsill to dry. If it kept its color, she would use it as part of a dried arrangement.

"Wish me luck," she whispered.

She wandered to her window and looked across the way. She searched his kitchen and his bedroom before she found him, in his den, bent over his desk. She sighed. Seeing David through the curtains was better than not seeing him at all.

She took one last glimpse of him, then got her coat and headed for the theater. It was time to pursue a dream.

On Tuesday night she got a call from the director.

"Rosalie, we want you for Nancy." She couldn't speak, her heart was pounding so. "Rosalie . . . are you still there?"

"I'm here. I just can't believe what I'm hearing."

"Believe it. We haven't heard a voice like yours on this stage in years. Where have you been hiding?"

"In the Edge of Paradise," she answered, laughing.

"Rehearsals start Thursday night. Seven sharp."

"I'll be there."

She hung up, then walked to her windowsill and picked up her rose. Holding it to her nose, she inhaled. Some of its sweet fragrance was still captured in the dried petals.

Gently, she set it back on the sill. "It's just you and me, rose. Withering around the edges but still hanging on."

Smiling, she went to her telephone. She had to tell David. She dialed information and got his number, then stood with the receiver in her hand.

Dreams deserved more than a telephone call.

Rosalie went to her closet and found her pink sweater. David would be home. He was always at home, out of reach behind his glass windows.

The wind caught her skirt and whipped it around her legs. It mussed her hair and bit her cheeks. She was shivering by the time she rang his front doorbell. She should have taken the time to get her winter coat.

She pressed the bell once more.

Inside, David made one last sweeping stroke on his watercolor, then went to the door. Rosalie was on his front porch, roses painting her cheeks and dreams dancing in her eyes.

"You'll be here six more weeks," she said.

"You got the part?"

"Yes."

"That's great." He held the door wider and pulled her inside. He hoped his unreasonable joy didn't show. "Come in. You're freezing."

"I forgot how cold it had turned." She pulled her pink sweater closer.

"I've built a fire. Why don't you sit in that chair and toast your feet. I'll get the wine."

"Wine?"

"For the celebration. You don't mind celebrating with cheap wine, do you?"

"I didn't expect to be celebrating at all."

Smiling, she sat in the chair beside the fire. The flames tinted her skin. His first urge was harmless; his second more dangerous. He wanted to strip off her clothes, arrange her on a quilt in front of the fire, and paint her; then he wanted to ravish her, inch by delicious inch, starting with the rosy skin on her cheeks and working his way down.

"I'll be right back with the wine," he said, escaping to the kitchen.

Rosalie sat in the chair until she felt toasty, then she glanced around the room. It was different from the last time she had been there—cozier. David had added a rocking chair and a small table. A colorful throw rug covered a portion of the scarred old hard-wood floor. An easel stood in the corner, and on it was one of the most beautiful paintings she had ever seen.

She left her chair to take a closer look. It was a watercolor, impressionistic flowers splashed against a luminous background. There was a brightness caught in the painting, as if the sun were woven into it.

Mesmerized, Rosalie stepped closer. It was the kind of painting that made you hold your breath.

"Do you like it?"

David was standing in the doorway, holding a bottle of wine in one hand and two empty glasses in the other. Rosalie let out her breath in a small whoosh.

"It's beautiful." She glanced back at the painting.

There was a signature in the corner. David's. "You did this?"

"It's a secret passion of mine."

"You shouldn't keep it a secret. It's magnificent."

"All my passions are secret."

For a sizzling moment his gaze held hers, and she longed to be one of his secret passions. At last he looked away from her and set the bottle on the fireside table.

"I'm not very good at this," she said.

"At what?" he said, handing her a glass of wine.

"Drinking. One glass makes me woozy, and two makes the room spin."

"Then we'll toast your success with hot chocolate."

"No." She sank into the fireside chair and tucked her feet under her, holding on to her wineglass. "I'm making a fresh start, trying things I've never tried, becoming a new woman."

"I liked the old one."

"You did?"

"I still do."

They sipped their wine, gazing at each other over the tops of their glasses.

"Tell me about your role," he said.

"I play Nancy. My role has some wonderful songs."

"Sing for me, Rosalie."

The wine had made her mellow. Softly, tenderly, she began to sing, "I'd Do Anything for You."

When the last note of the song faded away, she and David drank their wine, staring at each other with wonder and longing.

The level in the wine bottle steadily went down.

"You make me wish for things I can't have, Rosalie."

"So do you," she whispered.

The fire burned through a log, and it fell apart and sent a shower of sparks upward. David left his chair and got the poker. Leaning on the mantel, he stoked the fire. It gave him something to do with his hands.

The words of her song haunted him. She had not been singing merely *for* him, she had been singing *to* him. *Rosalie. Rosalie.* He couldn't let her fall in love with him. He couldn't fall in love with her. Love didn't survive around him.

Behind him, Rosalie's glass fell to the floor. David spun around. She was fast asleep, her head resting on the back of her chair and her feet tucked under her. The sound of her breathing was soft and even.

He squatted beside her. "Rosalie." She didn't stir. He put his hand on her arm. "Rosalie. Wake up." She didn't even flutter an eyelash.

She had told him she had no head for wine, and he had plied her with drink anyhow. She was a grown woman and knew what she was doing, but he should have insisted. He was, after all, a cop.

Her eyelashes were dark upon her cheeks, and the blue veins he loved so much pulsed softly in her throat. Tenderly, he traced them with his fingers.

"Why am I staying, Rosalie? Why am I playing with fire?"

His only answer was the even rise and fall of her breathing. He lifted her left hand and kissed each fingertip. She smiled in her sleep.

Would she be smiling if she knew where she was about to spend the night?

Gently, David lifted her into his arms and carried her to his bed.

Seven

She looked lush spread across his covers, lush and desirable. He sat on the side of the bed, staring at her. Her face was moist and flushed from wine and the warmth of the fire. A tiny bead of sweat dotted her upper lip. David bent over her and kissed it away.

Rosalie didn't stir.

With one finger he traced her eyebrows, her cheekbones, her mouth. She made soft, murmuring sounds, then fell back into a deep sleep with her lips parted. Tempted beyond reason, he placed his index finger against her lower lip, feeling the moist pink inner lining.

"You tempt me almost beyond enduring," he whispered as his finger moved inside her mouth with a steady, erotic rhythm.

He was so full with desire that he ached. The sound of his own blood was loud in his ears.

In her sleep she closed her mouth around his finger, sucking as if it were covered with pink sugar icing. He groaned and slowly withdrew his finger.

He should take her home. But that would mean

rousing her out of her sleep and carrying her out into the cold, then fishing around in her pocket to find her house key and traipsing through her house to her bedroom.

What difference did it make whether it was his bed or hers? Temptation would still stalk him.

She would spend the night at his house, on his bed, and he would keep watch over her in the straight-backed chair beside her in case she awakened and became disoriented and frightened.

It was a sensible plan.

Rosalie sighed in her sleep, then rolled to her side and curled one leg upward. The curve of hip and leg was intoxicating.

It was a dangerous plan.

She was wearing her clothes. He could undress her. There were a couple of reasons to take her clothes off and five dozen to leave them on.

David clenched his teeth and ran his hands through his hair. He would at least take off her shoes.

Bending down, he slid them from her feet. Blue veins showed in the arch, through her stockings. David pressed his lips to each curving arch, wetting the blue veins with his tongue.

He should take off her panty hose. They might constrict her breathing. He slid his hands up her legs, intent on his mission. Sweat beaded his upper lip and popped out on his brow. When his hands reached that soft, warm space between her thighs, he stepped back, cursing.

"You've had too damned much wine," he said to himself between clenched teeth.

She could sleep with her hose on; she could sleep with all her clothes on without suffering any harm. He hadn't been undressing her for her comfort; he'd been unveiling her for his pleasure.

He stalked to the closet and got a blanket, then carried it back to the bed and draped it over her, tucking it around her feet and under her chin. His breathing was harsh as he stood looking down at her.

"Rosalie, tonight I expect to pay for every sin I've ever committed."

His back rigid and all his muscles bunched so tightly it almost hurt to move, David went to the hard, uncomfortable chair and took up his watch. The night would be a lifetime of agony.

The blinding headache was what awakened her. Groaning, Rosalie struggled to open her eyes.

"Rosalie."

She jerked fully awake at the sound of her name. *David.* What was he doing in her bedroom?

"Rosalie, are you all right?" A chair scraped against the floor, and David was bending over her, holding his hand against her forehead.

He was so close in the dark, so close and so big and so real. If she was dreaming, she didn't ever want to wake up.

"David?" she whispered.

"I'm here, Rosalie. Everything is all right."

She caught hold of his hand and pulled herself upright. It hurt her head to move.

"What are you doing in my bedroom?"

"You're in *my* bedroom."

She flushed hot all the way down to the tip of her toes. In spite of a head that was three times too big for her body, she felt dreamy, wonderful.

"Did I . . . ? Did we . . . ?"

"You fell asleep by the fire. I tried to wake you, but you were sleeping too soundly."

"The wine." She bent her head down to rub her

aching temples. That's when she saw where his hand was. She was hanging on to it for dear life, pressing it against her breasts. Without warning, her nipples peaked and hardened. She sucked in a sharp breath. Would he notice?

"Yes, I think you had too much wine." He didn't move his hand, didn't try to enhance her already aroused state. Either he didn't notice or he was immune. "I take full responsibility for that, Rosalie. That's why I brought you here instead of taking you home . . . so I could watch over you."

She twisted her head and saw the hard chair pulled close to the bed. It was the only one in the room.

"You've been sitting there all night?"

"Yes."

"Sitting there awake, watching me sleep?"

"I think I dozed a couple of times."

It was then that Rosalie knew she loved him. Groaning softly, she pressed his hand close to her heart. Life was a prankster. Love was supposed to come riding in on a white charger with banners unfurled, not sneak in the back door while she dreamed. Love was supposed to be announced with music and roses, not with a hangover and wrinkled clothes that had been slept in.

"Are you all right? Can I get you something?"

"An aspirin, please. I have a terrible headache."

David left the room swiftly. Rosalie pulled the blanket around her shoulders, shivering. There *had* been music and roses, music sung from the heart and one perfect rose given from the soul.

"Oh, David, David," she whispered. "What am I going to do?"

A tear rolled down her cheek, and she angrily brushed it away. No tears for her. She was going to be strong this time, strong and brave and wise.

"I brought you two. And a glass of water." David sat on the edge of the bed, handed her the aspirin, and held the glass to her lips.

She drank. The water was cool going down, but his hand on her chin was hot, hot with the passion that always rose between them so quickly, so unexpectedly.

"Thank you," she said.

He took the glass away and set it on the bedside table. Then he got off the bed and sat down in his awful chair.

"What time is it?" she asked.

"Almost two."

"I should go home."

"It's cold outside . . . and raining."

"Are you going to stay there . . . in the chair?"

"Yes. You might need me again."

I need you now, David, lying beside me with your arms wrapped around me.

"If you're going to sit on that hard chair the rest of the night, I'm going home." She bit her lower lip. "I probably should anyhow."

"Nothing is going to happen, Rosalie. I promise you that."

Did he know how she felt? Could he tell? Did it show in her eyes?

"That's the least of my worries," she said, trying to sound breezy. "What I am worried about is you sitting in that hard chair. It's not good for your back."

He smiled. "Are you trying to tell me I'm not young?"

"Well . . . are you?"

"No. Forty."

"That settles it then." With a bravado she was far from feeling, Rosalie scooted to the far side of the bed and patted the mattress. "Hop in. No need to remove your clothes. It would break a pattern."

"The chair is fine."

"Don't be foolish, David. We're both adults. You're perfectly safe with me." He arched one eyebrow. "Not tonight, honey," she teased. "I have a headache."

He laughed. "Rosalie, you're the damnedest woman." His shoes hit the floor with a plop. "That's twice you've conned me."

"Wait till the next time, mister." She stretched out on her side of the bed, drew the blanket up to her chin, and tried to look calm. The bed creaked and the mattress sagged when David climbed in on the other side, fully dressed except for his shoes and his belt.

"Good night, Rosalie," he said, turning his back to her and pulling his half of the covers up to his waist.

"Good night."

In spite of being up most of the night, David woke early. Rosalie was curled against him, one arm draped over his waist, one leg wedged between his, and her enticing curves pressed into his back.

It would be so easy to roll over and gather her into his arms, so easy to kiss her, so easy to get her to kiss him. They were already in the bed. If they got started, there would be no stopping this time.

David clenched his jaw against the passion that threatened to unseat his reason. Gently, so as not to wake her, he eased her hand off his waist. That small task was relatively painless.

Unwrapping himself from her body was the hard part. He suffered a thousand regrets as he untangled himself from her exquisite legs.

The mattress squeaked as he eased off the bed. David cursed silently. Finally, he was upright, standing beside the bed looking down at her. His breath came in short, harsh gasps.

Rosalie slept on, curved sweetly upon his bed, her hair spread upon his pillow and her hips pressed into the warm spot where he had been. He was either a fool to leave her or the most noble man God ever put upon the earth.

Moving in the pale half-light of dawn, David tiptoed around the bed and found his shoes. He didn't slip them on until he was outside the bedroom door.

"Narrow escape," he whispered, leaning against the doorframe.

When his breathing returned to normal, he went into the kitchen to make breakfast for two.

Joy zinged through Rosalie when she woke up, and she didn't understand why until she looked at the pillow next to hers. It was dented. Two in the bed together. It had felt so good.

Smiling in spite of a slight twinge in her head, she got out of David's bed and made what repairs she could in his bathroom. Her clothes and her face both looked as if they had been slept in.

She was too happy to care.

She found him in the kitchen, setting out orange juice for two.

"You made breakfast for me?"

"Good morning, Rosalie." He pulled out a chair at the table. "I thought you'd have time for a big breakfast before you leave for work. It should be a welcome change from cereal."

"How did you know?"

"Detective work."

Spying through the windows. She'd done a lot of it herself.

"You're sweet to do this, David." Rosalie sat in the

chair he offered, and had breakfast with the man she loved. The only problem was that he didn't love her back.

After she left his house, David headed toward the shower. On the way through his bedroom he passed by the bed. Her fragrance lingered there, and the covers still bore the impression of her body.

He picked up her pillow and pressed it to his face, inhaling. Need washed over him, need and desire so great, he groaned aloud.

"Dammitall." He threw the pillow onto the bed and stalked into the shower. The water he turned on was cold.

David stood at his window watching Rosalie leave for rehearsals. It had been one week since she'd come to his house, one week since she'd slept in his bed, one week since he had felt her body pressed close to his.

It felt like an eternity.

He left the window and went to his easel. Rover padded along behind him, wagging his tail and smiling his doggie smile.

He was going to have to do something about that dog. In five more weeks he'd be leaving. As soon as he saw Rosalie's stage debut, he would pull out of Tupelo and move on to another place, a town that didn't put him too close to the edge of paradise.

David picked up his brush and began to paint.

Rosalie sat in the theater with the rest of the cast, wondering if she was, after all, too old for the stage. Rehearsals were long, and the director was demanding. She barely had time to squeeze everything into her day—work, memorizing lines and songs, rehearsals.

The only good thing about the frenzied activity was that she didn't have time to think about how much she missed David.

"Listen up, cast." Dennis Gossoway, the director, held up his hands for attention. "We'll start building and painting the set tomorrow night. Our backstage crew is terrific, but we can always use more hands. If any of you have time to help with the set, or if you know of anyone who does, let me know."

Wayne Evans, who was playing the Artful Dodger, raised his hand. "I'm handy with a hammer. I'll help with the carpentry."

"Good. Anybody else? BJ Nanney will paint the backdrop, but he's always looking for help. Anybody here happen to be an artist?"

Rosalie raised her hand. "I know someone."

She decided bribery was her best bet. When she got home from rehearsals, she laid out the plates, the napkins, the silver, and the apple pie. Then she picked up the phone.

He answered on the first ring.

"David? I know it's late, but I saw your light on and thought you might still be up."

"Rosalie? How's it going?"

"Great."

"I'm glad," he said.

Both of them went silent.

She hung on to the phone, wishing. Even the sound of his breathing on the other end of the line made her want him.

"David . . . I wonder if you could come over."

"Now?"

"If it's not too much trouble."

"I'll be right there."

By the time she had hung up the phone and freshened her lipstick, he was at her door.

"Come in, I have pie waiting."

"Sounds good. I haven't had a taste of anything sweet in a long time."

She poured coffee for two, then sat at the table and served the pie.

"You look good," he said.

"You too."

They ate in silence, stealing glances at each other at every opportunity. When the air was so thick and heavy with thwarted passion, Rosalie thought she might stop breathing, she left the table and began to pace.

"Something's on your mind," he said. "Is anything wrong?"

"I hope not." She folded her hands together, then came to stand beside him, not close enough to touch but close enough so she could look into his eyes. "There's something I want you to do for me, David."

"I'd do anything for you, Rosalie."

She smiled. "That sounds like my song."

"I listen to you practice. I guess the song's on my mind."

Am I? Am I on your mind as much as you are on mine?

"Tomorrow night we start building and painting the set for *Oliver!*" David's jaw tensed, but he didn't interrupt. "I told them you would help."

"No." The chair scraped against the kitchen floor as he stood up. "I'm sorry, Rosalie. I can't do it."

"Can't or won't?"

"Does it make any difference?"

"Yes."

"I'd do anything for you, Rosalie. You know that."

"Except this?"

"Except this. I'm sorry."

"Why, David?"

"I don't want to form connections in this town. I'm leaving in five weeks, and when I go, I want it to be a clean break."

"Nobody left behind to mourn your going?"

His expression was fierce as he came to her. She didn't back away. He cupped her face, ever so gently, barely touching her skin.

"I can't make commitments, Rosalie. Not to the theater, not to Rover, not to . . . anyone."

Her love was without a future. Rosalie knew it then. She guessed she'd always known it. The knowledge settled into her heart like a thorn, but it didn't stop her from loving him.

"David . . ." She took one of his hands between hers, cradling it with exquisite tenderness. "I meant to bribe you with pie. I was even thinking of ways I could blackmail you—by telling you that I had given a promise and if you didn't go, my word would be worthless." She laced her fingers with his and held their entwined hands to her cheeks. "Seeing you now, seeing the pain in your eyes, I don't ask that you do this for me. I ask that you do it for yourself."

"Rosalie . . ."

"Shhh . . ." She placed her free hand over his lips. "You can't run forever, David. I know you can't come back in one giant step, but I'm asking you to start back with one small step . . . just one."

David ached. He ached with tenderness and desire and guilt.

"I'll be going when it's over," he said.

"I know that." She smiled. "Thank you, David."

"How did you know I was going to say yes?"

"Your eyes already said it."

"You're a sorceress, Rosalie."

"If I were a sorceress, I would cast you under my spell."

"You already have."

With their hands laced together, they gazed at each other, naked longing in their eyes. Rosalie flicked her tongue over her bottom lip. David stood staunch, dying a little inside.

Eight

The capricious Mississippi weather had turned
warm again, so that November felt almost like
spring. David and Rosalie formed a habit of walking
to the theater together. While she was onstage re-
hearsing, he was offstage, helping construct a village
in Dickens's England.

Dialogue was carried on amid the hammering and
sawing, but when the actors sang, all carpentry
ceased. Most of the set crew stepped outside to
smoke, but David moved to the darkened wings of
the stage to watch Rosalie.

She had always been a beautiful woman, lovely to
look at, lovely to touch, but onstage she was trans-
formed. He stood in the wings, enchanted.

Her voice soared through the theater. David pretended she was singing for him alone, as she had the
night she had come to his house to announce that
she had the role.

Then, afterward, walking home with her in the
dark, he liked to believe that there was such a thing
as redemption.

"Next week is Thanksgiving, David," she said,

swinging their joined hands as they made their way home.

It was late, almost eleven o'clock, and the moon was hiding behind a dark cloud that foreboded rain. But David didn't have to see her face to know what it looked like: He had it memorized.

"I hadn't noticed."

"Then you obviously don't have plans."

"No, I don't. I never celebrate Thanksgiving."

"Why not? Or is that too personal?"

They were passing under a streetlight. All the sweetness and warmth of her personality shone in her face. How could he deny her anything?

"We never had money for a turkey when I was growing up. And then later . . . after I married Gretchen, it seemed I was always on duty. We never developed the habit of celebrating holidays."

"Even Christmas?"

"At first we did. But after it became clear that there was nothing left between us, we didn't even bother to go through the motions." She tilted her face up toward his. He wanted to kiss her. "Gifts should come from the heart, Rosalie."

Rosalie remembered the rose he had given her. It was time to give him something in return.

"Come to Thanksgiving dinner at my house, David."

"Thank you, but . . ."

"Please?" She put her hand over his lips. "Don't say no."

"You'll have your family. Your boys will be home from school. I don't want to intrude on that."

"You won't be intruding. I always invite Betty. She has no family."

"You have the kind of heart that takes in strays, Rosalie."

"I take in friends."

He caught both her hands and stood facing her under the streetlamp.

"Is that what we are? Friends?"

He saw the slight tremor that went through her, felt it in her hands. He tightened his hold, pulling her closer.

"I think we're more than friends, David."

"So do I, Rosalie." He tipped her chin upward with the back of his hand. With eyes as bright and bottomless as a blue summer sky, Rosalie wet her bottom lip with the tip of her tongue. She was so close . . . so close he could feel the contours of her soft and inviting body gently brushing against him. "We are more than friends, much more."

She moved closer, standing on tiptoe so that her lips were only a whisper away.

"I can handle that, David."

"I can, too . . . as long as you're not in my house and I'm not in yours."

Her cheeks flushed with memories. "I don't serve wine. I won't end up in your bed."

"I'll make sure that doesn't happen again." Her face never lost its lovely glow. "Don't you see, Rosalie? It's more than that, more than the possibility you'll end up in my bed. . . . It's the possibility that you'll end up in my heart. I can't let that happen."

"I don't know why that makes me sad, but it does."

Her warm, sweet breath caressed his lips, his cheeks. David held on to her, flirting with temptation and cursing fate.

"Don't be sad, Rosalie. Not over me."

She sighed, then stepped back. David released her, feeling a powerful sense of loss.

"If you change your mind, David . . . about the turkey . . . come on over."

"I won't change my mind."

A restraint came over them, as if they had both

attended the burial of a dear friend and didn't know how to shed tears over his passing. By mutual consent they didn't hold hands the rest of the way home.

When they reached her front door, Rosalie turned to David. "Tomorrow night, David?"

He almost told her no . . . for both their sakes. Then he pictured her walking the dark streets to the theater alone.

"Tomorrow night," he said, knowing he would be there only a few more weeks. He could be strong that long.

Thanksgiving arrived with bluster. There was a nip of frost in the air and a strong, hard wind that wrestled the few dry leaves in the oak tree to the ground.

Inside her house, Rosalie put the turkey into the oven, then looked out her window. A single light burned in David's house, in his kitchen.

"What are you looking at, Mom?" Jack came up behind her and gave her a bear hug. "That old squirrel?"

"No. My neighbor, David Kelly. I invited him to Thanksgiving dinner."

"Good. I enjoy a big crowd." Jack got the milk jug out of the refrigerator and the cereal from the top shelf, reaching it easily without a stool. Rosalie was proud of how tall her sons were, tall and sturdy and noble.

She busied herself with congealed salad and green-bean casserole while Jack dug into his breakfast with the huge appetite of the young.

"Is he anybody special?" Jack's casual question caught her off guard.

"Who, dear?" she asked, buying a little time with her pretended ignorance.

"*Dear?* Good grief, Mom. You sound like one of those antiquated television shows. *Father Knows Best.*"

Rosalie dried her hands on the dish towel, then poured herself a cup of coffee and joined her son at the table.

"He's special, Jack. But there's nothing between us."

Jack covered her hand with his. "It's okay, Mom. You're a beautiful woman. Men are bound to notice you. Just be careful, that's all."

"He's not like Harry. I'm certain of that."

"Jimmy and I were too young to do anything about Harry, but we're grown men now. Nothing like that will ever happen to you again. We'll make sure of that."

Rosalie laughed.

"What's so funny, Mom?" asked Jimmy, coming into the kitchen, stretching and yawning. He was the late bloomer, the late sleeper.

"All this time I thought I was taking care of the two of you." She got up to give Jimmy a hug. "Now it seems that the two of you are taking care of me."

"Fine by me. Who do you want killed?" Snarling, he got into a boxing stance, then punched the air three times.

"I was just telling Mom how grown up we are, but you blew it, Ace."

"It was temporary childhood regression, that's all." Jimmy scooped up the cereal box, then grabbed a bowl from the cabinet. "Boy, it's good to be home." He sniffed the air. "Just smell all that home cooking. Turkey, dressing, apple pie."

"Did I hear somebody say apple pie?" Betty breezed into the kitchen without knocking, bearing a basketful of pies, her annual contribution to the Thanksgiving meal.

Jack and Jimmy left their places at the table to give her big hugs. She pinched their cheeks and squeezed their arms.

"If you two get any handsomer, I'm going to have to follow you down to school to beat the girls off with a baseball bat."

"Jack's got one that needs beating off. She covers him like white on rice."

"Speak for yourself, Ace."

Rosalie joined the lively banter, but her heart was only half in it. Across the way a single light burned in a lonely kitchen.

David told himself he wasn't going. He even told Rover he wasn't going.

"No point in getting worked up over Thanksgiving." He opened a can of dog food and poured it in Rover's dish. "The two of us will do just fine, won't we, boy?" Rover thumped his tail in agreement. "Who needs a family? Right, boy?" The dog's tail whacked the floor. "Just because she's sweet and soft and gentle . . . that's no reason to break a long-standing tradition, eh, Rover?"

Rover, heavily involved in his gourmet meal, ignored the question.

David wandered over to his window. Rosalie's tall sons were helping her in the kitchen. They moved back and forth with china plates, while Betty stirred something in a big pot on the stove.

David wondered if it was giblet gravy. He'd had it one Thanksgiving down at the station. He and Hubert Franklin had been on duty, and Hubert's wife had brought dinner down, turkey with all the trimmings, including giblet gravy. Franklin had said it was a dying art, making that gravy.

David stood at his window, looking into Rosalie's kitchen but seeing inside his soul. Not even one glimmer of light relieved the stark blackness in that yawning void.

Suddenly, he found himself staring into Rosalie's eyes. She was at her window, the curtain clutched in her hand. His heart slammed against his chest, and sweat gathered on his upper lip in spite of the chill.

Then Rosalie lowered the curtain and was gone. David walked away from the window, watching his warped floor so he wouldn't trip in the cracks.

Rosalie delayed the meal as long as she could. Finally, it was clear to her that David was not coming.

"Let's eat," she said.

"I thought you were never going to say that, Mom," Jimmy said. "I'm starving."

"You're always starving," Jack told his brother. As he held Rosalie's chair, he leaned down and whispered, "I'm sorry about the neighbor, Mom."

"Thanks." She patted his hand.

Jack had already carved the turkey when the knock came at the door. Betty arched her eyebrows; Jack looked at Rosalie, and Jimmy pushed back his chair.

"I'll get it, Mom," he said.

"No. Wait." She touched her throat with one hand and felt the pulse beating wildly there. "I will."

"Is it too late?" David asked when she opened the door.

"No, David. It's never too late."

She led him to the table and introduced him to Betty and her sons.

• • •

"Shoot, Jack, did you see the way they looked at each other?"

"So. What's the crime in looking?"

Jack and Jimmy were in the back seat of Shine Jenkin's car, heading south toward Baton Rouge and the big post-Thanksgiving football game between their school and LSU.

"Yeah, but he stayed to wash the dishes."

"Mom can use the help."

"I don't think he had washing dishes on his mind, Jack."

Shine Jenkins grinned at them over his shoulder. "Do you dudes mind if I turn up the radio? All this soap-opera stuff is putting me to sleep."

"Go ahead and turn it up, Shine," Jimmy said, "but if you keep it on that bluegrass station, I'm going to puke."

"Regurgitate, man. Haven't you learned a thing at college?" Shine found a country-western station and turned it up loud enough to rattle the windows. Then he yelled over the music, "If it's that big dude I saw at your house when I picked you up that's got you worried, I think you can put it out of your mind."

"Why is that?" Jimmy asked, leaning over the front seat so Shine could hear.

"I saw him on that television show, you know that thing with Donna Frensberg? He was being cited for uncommon bravery or some such thing in that big bank holdup over in Red Bay about three years ago." Shine blew a big bubble with his gum, then popped it. "He's not one of those slicked-up television cops. He's a real hero, man."

Rosalie washed and David dried. Standing by his side at her kitchen sink, she passed the dishes to him. Every now and then her soapy hands touched his, and his hip brushed against hers. The room was alive with sexual currents.

"Your sons are fine young men," David said. "I'm sorry they had to leave so soon after dinner."

"It's a long drive, and they wanted to be there for all the pregame parties." Rosalie delved into the soapsuds and came up with the last china plate. Soon the dishes would be finished, and David would be going. If she were a clever modern woman, schooled in the art of seduction, she could make him stay. Unfortunately, she was just an ordinary woman, schooled in the art of survival.

Sighing, she passed him the last plate. His hand covered hers and lingered. Her breath caught high in her throat.

"You'll get slippery," she said. They looked at each other, then got lost in a long, searching gaze. Rosalie cleared her throat. ". . . from the soap, I mean."

His eyes were as hot as blue flames, and his face was tight with passion. He took the plate from her slowly and set it aside.

"I know what you mean, Rosalie."

She licked her lips. "It was kind of you to stay and help with the dishes. Generous."

"It was neither generous nor kind. It was selfish. I wanted to be with you." Taking up the dishcloth, he moved apart so that they were no longer touching.

Rosalie wanted to scream. Instead, she made conversation.

"Betty usually does this. I think she invented that chore she had to hurry home and do." She reached for the ribbon in her hair. The sleeves she had rolled to do dishes slid back, exposing her upper arms.

David stared at that fine lacing of pale blue veins pulsing just underneath her fair skin. "I've run out of things to invent, Rosalie, reasons to stay away."

"Then don't . . . don't stay away."

"The turkey was delicious, the giblet gravy wonderful . . . but I think I came here today to see this." He traced the path of veins on her upper arm with his index finger.

She wondered how long she could live holding her breath. His hand was hot on her arm, hot and tender and sexy. She thought she might faint if he didn't take his hand away, and she knew she would die if he did.

"You are so soft," David said, lingering over the touch. "So fair." He leaned down and trailed his lips along her upper arm.

Desire exploded through her so fast and hard, she trembled.

"Yes," she whispered, reaching for him. "Oh, yes."

David caught her against his chest and held her close, his heart thundering against hers, his body heat searing her. He was tight and hard with tension as he sought to hold back. A groan escaped his lips.

They were both beyond control, and they both knew it.

"I want you, David . . . here . . . now. . . ."

"Rosalie . . ."

"Nothing else matters. Nothing but this."

They came together in a fury of passion. His kisses were hard and demanding, hers wild and wanton. His hand slid up her skirt, and she wrapped one leg around him. They rocked together, mouths tightly melded.

Years of denial made them desperate. The depth of their passion made them bold.

"Please . . . David . . . please. . . "

He answered her plea. The small wisp of silk separating them was pushed aside. He lifted her up and braced her against the kitchen sink; then, in one powerful thrust, he entered her.

There was nothing kind or sweet or sentimental

about their lovemaking. The waiting had been too long, the wanting too desperate. She dug her hands into his shoulders, leaving marks on his skin through his shirt; and he gripped her hips and drove at her without mercy.

With David buried deep in her, Rosalie cast her last shred of civilized behavior aside. In language she might later think about and consider shocking, she told him what she liked, what she wanted, what she had to have.

And he joyfully obliged. He plundered her mouth until it felt puffy and bruised, suckled her breasts until they felt ready to burst. He moved his hands over her, stroking, exploring, igniting.

All the years of keeping her sexual self hidden fell by the wayside, and Rosalie went up in flames. She gave herself more fully, more completely, to David than she had to any other man. What she had with him there at her kitchen sink with the soapy water sloshing over her hips and running down her legs was a mature love, a totally adult experience.

They rode the thundering horse of passion until they reached their destination, that high, bright place on the edge of the world where everything seemed unreal and at the same time so magnificently defined that it hurt to look.

She leaned her head against David's shoulder, and he wove his hands into her damp hair. Gently, she kissed the skin exposed at the neck of his shirt. A tremor ran through him.

It was such a small thing. A tremor. And yet it told Rosalie more than a million words. David was moved by her, moved to the point that one tender touch racked his whole body. If that wasn't love, it was enough to suffice.

"Rosalie?"

She didn't lift her head, didn't move, couldn't move.

"It was beautiful, David. Let's not spoil it with words."

He held on to her, clung to her as if he were drifting at sea and she were the only lifeline in sight. What he had done was unconscionable. He had taken her like an animal, without thought of her future. She was not the kind of woman a man could use and then discard. She was not a modern-day woman accustomed to casual one-night stands.

Rosalie deserved more. She deserved a man who would pledge vows at an altar and then move heaven and earth to keep those vows . . . and he could never be that man.

He held on to her so tightly, his arms trembled, and he was ashamed.

She brushed her lips lightly over his neck once more, and he groaned in agony. Walking away this time was going to be worse than death: It was going to an act that would torture him the rest of his life.

Tenderly, he released her, silently praying that she would understand, that she wouldn't be hurt, desperately hoping that he was doing the right thing, the noble thing.

When they were standing slightly apart with the soapy water puddling at their feet, he adjusted their clothes, then traced her lips with his index finger.

"I hope you can forgive me, Rosalie, for I can never forgive myself."

He left quickly, unable to endure the light of her eyes. Without turning back, he went through her kitchen door, closing it carefully behind him.

Rosalie stared at the closed door, wishing she were the kind of woman who could kick furniture and scream. Was it possible to be gloriously, blissfully happy, and painfully, horribly sad at the same time?

Her cheeks and her body still burned with the heat of passion. She felt released, rescued, *saved*. And yet her heart was breaking into a million pieces.

She kept staring at the door, hoping it would open, hoping David would walk back inside and say, "I've changed my mind, Rosalie. I can't experience what we had and just walk away."

The door stayed shut. She clenched her hands into fists, willing it to open, daring it to open.

Still it remained closed.

"David, David," she whispered.

She wrapped her arms around herself, whimpering like a whipped kitten. Scenes from her past flashed before her eyes, and she saw herself, an actress upon the stage of life, getting trapped in one circumstance after another.

The old clock on the wall marked time with a loud ticking; and when Rosalie finally became aware of her surroundings, she was surprised to discover how late it was, how long she had been standing in the kitchen.

She leaned toward her window and stared across the way. A light was burning in David's bedroom. Was he sprawled on top of the covers, fast asleep, worn out and sated from their lovemaking?

No, that wasn't fair. He had been in great pain when he'd left. She'd seen it in his eyes, felt it in the way he touched her face.

She stared at his bedroom window while the clock on the wall recorded the marching of time. Rosalie was not a young woman anymore—and David would soon be gone.

She hurried to her bathroom, shedding clothes as she went and leaving them in a messy trail on the floor. Tomorrow she would be neat; tonight she was going to be bold.

After her bath, she dressed in fresh jeans and

T-shirt, then grabbed a sweater and went into the night. It was very late, but the light in David's bedroom still burned.

She went through his backyard and climbed the back-porch steps. David hadn't even locked his door. Somehow that gave her hope, that he had been so upset, he had forgotten to lock his door.

She eased through and found her way to his bedroom in the dark. He was lying on top of his covers, still wearing his jeans and tennis shoes, his hands laced behind his head, staring up at the ceiling.

She leaned against the doorway, hungry with the need to observe him, desperate with the desire to touch him. His broad chest rose and fell with his harsh breathing. The lines of his body were tight and hard with tension.

She knew he was in turmoil; otherwise she would never have gained his bedroom door without his knowledge. He was a cop. Experience and training would have made him alert under ordinary circumstances.

She was hopeful that these were not ordinary circumstances.

She held on to the doorframe until her knuckles were white. She didn't move, barely breathed.

David's naked chest was magnificent, beautiful. His muscles were sculpted, finely defined. He was hard and tanned and smooth. His chest hairs were dark and mysterious, swirling in an enticing pattern toward the top of his jeans.

Rosalie longed. She dreamed. She wanted.

Was she a female Peeping Tom, standing in his bedroom doorway uninvited and unannounced? She was just getting ready to make herself known when David moved.

Slowly, he turned his head. His eyes were still dark with passion. He didn't move, didn't speak.

She clung to the door.

When it seemed that she was going to fall off the razor edge of time and be sliced in half, David spoke.

"Why did you come?"

"Because I want you."

He got off the bed and moved to the window. She saw the long, angry scar that slashed his back. She wasn't aware of making a sound, but David whirled around, his eyes blazing.

"My soul is just as ugly, Rosalie. I'm marked, scarred. You deserve better."

"No!" She wanted to run to him, to gather him in her arms and hold him. Instinct kept her standing in the door. "You are good, David, good and kind and noble."

He balled his hands into fists and rammed them in his pockets. "Don't you think I want you, Rosalie? Don't you know that I'd give my soul to be free, to have the right to come to you boldly, to court you, to take you places you deserve to be, fancy places with snooty waiters and expensive wine and cloth napkins?"

She made a step toward him, but he held up his hand.

"Please. If you touch me, I can't promise to resist."

"Then don't."

"Rosalie . . ."

She came to him then, bold and certain. Wrapping her arms around his waist, she leaned her head on his bare chest.

"I'm not asking for a commitment, David. I know you're leaving."

"Yes. I am." Though his body was still stiff with resistance, his hands settled lightly on her shoulders.

She took hope. "All I'm asking for is a brief and lovely interlude, something we can remember when you go back to Alabama and I go back to the business of getting my sons through school."

His mind might be resisting, but his body was betraying him. Rosalie moved closer, moved into that great, thundering passion that was rising in him.

"Don't you see, David? All my life I've let myself get carried by whatever current came along. This time I'm breaking the pattern, doing something for myself, merely because I want to." She tipped her head back so she could see his face. "You don't have to be in love with me. You don't have to want me as much as I want you. . . ."

"I do, Rosalie. More." He wove his hands into her hair. "I've wanted you from the first day I saw you, from the moment you lifted your arms and I saw that tiny network of blue veins on your soft skin." He pressed a tender kiss on her forehead. "I've stood at my window dreaming how it would be with you in my arms, in my bed."

Smiling, she turned her head toward his bed.

"There it is, David. . . . And here I am."

He tightened his hold and buried his face in her hair. "I wish I could make promises, Rosalie. . . ."

"I don't need them."

Silently, they swayed together, her heart clamoring against his and his breath mingling with hers.

"I have to be the luckiest man alive," he said as he lifted her with exquisite care.

The bed loomed before them, cracked and chipped and old, with the faded covers bleached pure and white in the moonlight. They were in a magical place. Both of them felt it.

He negotiated his way across the room, toward that bright and shining bed. He felt as if he were carrying a miracle. When they reached their destination, he lowered her to the covers, then leaned over her, studying her face.

She smiled at him.

He had come to Tupelo battered and bruised, seeking another place to hide; but this lovely, gentle woman had poured balm over his spirit and unlocked the doors to his prison. Little by little, she was coaxing him out to freedom.

"We have three weeks, Rosalie."

"Let's make them all count."

Nine

This time was different. Their passion was just as intense, but their loving was slow and easy. They undressed each other, taking time to marvel, to caress, to kiss.

When she lay across his bed with her bare skin gleaming in the moonlight, he put on music, Domingo singing "O Paradis." Then he stood over the bed, marveling.

"You are beautiful," he said, trailing one finger from her throat to the warm cleft between her thighs. "I want to paint you."

"Like this?" She blushed, suddenly shy.

"Yes. Like this." He lay down beside her and drew her into his arms. "But first I want to kiss you."

He kissed her with such tenderness, she thought she had drifted upward and joined the rejoicing angels in paradise. She clung to him, giving her heart, her soul, while the magnificent voice of Domingo washed over them.

"And I want to kiss you," she whispered when they stopped for breath.

Gently, she pushed him onto his back. Her fragrance drifted over him as she nibbled his neck.

"You smell like roses," he said.

She moved lower, burying her lips in the swirl of hairs on his chest. "Do you like roses, David?"

"I'm crazy about them. . . ."

Her warm tongue dipped into his navel, then left a hot trail down his abdomen. Opera music soared, and so did David.

"Rosalie . . . Rosalie." He spoke her name as both prayer and plea.

Still sweet, still tender, Rosalie took him into her mouth and carried him over the edge of the world. It was a beautiful gift of the heart, one he would cherish forever.

Music and love and moonlight and roses blended together until Rosalie and David didn't know where one ended and the other began. With lips and hands they pleasured each other, and when that was no longer enough, they came together for that long, slow sweet ride to ecstasy.

And afterward, they fell asleep wrapped in each other's arms.

Friday morning he painted her. She was in bed, freshly wakened with the blush of loving still on her skin. Her hair was in sexy disarray, and her eyes were luminous with joy.

David's brush flew across the easel. "You're a great model, Rosalie. Natural, unselfconscious."

"You deserve all the credit."

He laughed. It was so good to hear him laugh. In all the time she'd known him, she had never seen David so open, so relaxed.

"Do we do all this in one sitting?"

"We can unless you get tired. With watercolors the painting goes faster."

He bent over his work, intense, absorbed. She loved watching him paint, loved the way his hands moved. It was almost as if he were making love to the canvas.

Rover padded in to investigate, stopping long enough to sniff David's legs, then padded out again. The squirrel outside their window set up a chattering, scolding the blue jay who had swooped down to quarrel over territory.

It was a lovely sunshiny morning, the kind of morning she and David might have if they were married. *Married*. The word settled in her mind like a promise. David was strong and tender, fierce and kind, a complex man she could spend the rest of her life loving.

Her mind drifted with the promise as if it were true, and then she came crashing back to reality. They had three weeks. That was all.

"What's wrong, Rosalie?"

How could she tell him the truth? That she was sad thinking that they would never truly belong to each other?

"I suppose I'm getting hungry."

"Then let's eat breakfast." He began to put away his art supplies. "I can finish the painting later."

"But won't it be different? I mean, I need to wash my face and comb my hair and put on my clothes before I eat."

"You're right, Rosalie." His eyes danced with devilment as he sat on the edge of the bed and cupped her face. "I guess I'll just have to muss you up again."

She pretended to give the idea deep thought. With barely suppressed laughter, she pulled back the covers.

"That could take a long time, David."

"You're right again." He shed his jeans and climbed under the covers. "I guess I'd better start now."

They romped like children all day Friday. Rosalie delighted in giving David the first real holiday he'd ever had, and he exulted in giving her all the simple pleasures of courtship she'd missed.

After breakfast he rigged a swing in the backyard and pushed her as high as the ropes would go. Her laughter was his reward. When she had swung until her cheeks were rosy, they walked hand in hand to the corner grocery.

"Close your eyes, Rosalie," he said as he separated a cart from the line. "I want to surprise you."

"If you wanted to surprise me, why didn't I stay home?"

"Because I can't bear to be without you."

The day they would say good-bye loomed in their minds, but they laughed and pretended it didn't exist.

"How can I see to walk?" she asked, closing her eyes.

"I'll lead you." He took her hand. "Do you trust me, Rosalie?"

"Always, David."

Laughing, they moved up one aisle and down the other, with David putting items into the cart and Rosalie trying to guess what they were.

"Cabbage," she said.

"Do you think I would serve cabbage to a princess?"

"Bananas?"

"Bananas are for monkeys." He led her down the

aisle and stopped at the snacks. "Don't look, Rosalie, but there are two women staring at us."

"What do they look like?"

"One looks like a bowling ball with a ponytail, and the other looks like Elmer Fudd with lipstick."

Rosalie chuckled. "Grace Crowley and Mildred Martin. Smile and wave at them, David. I want them to be sure and see you."

Keeping his hold on Rosalie, David smiled at the two women. Then, for good measure, he waved.

"What are they doing now, David?"

"Pretending they haven't been staring at us for the last five minutes."

"Can I peek?"

"Only if you don't look into the cart."

Rosalie opened one eye. Mildred and Grace had turned their backs and were loudly discussing the merits of potato chips versus corn chips, but every now and then they cast furtive glances over their shoulders.

Rosalie caught their eye and waved.

Overcome by curiosity, Mildred and Grace hurried toward Rosalie.

"Here they come," David said. "Don't look in the cart, Rosalie."

"My goodness, Rosalie," Mildred said, holding her hand over her panting heart. "What a surprise to see you." She glanced significantly toward David. "You must have had out-of-town relatives for Thanksgiving."

"No. This is David Kelly, my new neighbor."

"A neighbor?" Arching her eyebrows, Grace looked down at Rosalie's hand, nestling in David's.

While Rosalie was thinking how she might goad them next, David intervened. He turned on the charm. Within minutes he had Mildred and Grace almost purring. Rosalie watched, fascinated. It was a side of David she had never seen.

"What was that all about?" he asked after the two women had left.

"They've been speculating about my merry widowhood since Harry died. I wanted to give them something new to talk about, but I think you charmed them right out of their viciousness."

"That was the general idea. Sometimes a little charm defuses a situation."

"You must be a good cop."

He grew very still, gazing into the distance. "I was . . . once."

Back home David instructed Rosalie to sit by the fire while he unloaded his surprise groceries.

"I want to make lunch for you," he said.

"You made breakfast."

"I want to spoil you."

She kissed him soundly on the lips, then went to sit on the rug beside the fire. She felt pampered, loved.

"Close your eyes, Rosalie," David called from the hallway. Smiling, she closed her eyes. The old floor squeaked as he came toward her. China plates rattled as he set the tray in front of the fire. "You can open your eyes now. Lunch is served." It was three o'clock in the afternoon. "Or we could call it dinner."

The tray was filled with every kind of forbidden goody children dream about, chocolate and whipped cream and marshmallows and strawberries and oranges and ice cream and butterscotch syrup.

She clapped her hands, smiling.

"If any of your favorites are missing, I'll jog back to the store to get them."

"You're the only thing that's missing." Rosalie

pulled him down beside her, then ran her hands over his chest. "You feel so nice."

"I'm even better with strawberries." He held one between his lips and offered it to her. She ate the first strawberry that way, and the second, and the third.

On the fourth she stopped to sample his lips. Then she sampled him with whipped cream. "Hmmm. Better and better," she murmured. "But I want more."

"Anything, Rosalie. You can have anything you want."

She reached for his shirt buttons. "I'm yearning for fruit salad . . . with chocolate." Boldly, she stripped aside his shirt, then pressed both palms flat over his chest.

Blood roared in his ears, and desire tightened his loins. In how many ways did he want her? he wondered. And how many times? They had loved in his tumbled bed with the early morning sun pouring over them, then later in the kitchen with her cheeks rosy from swinging. He had wanted her in the grocery store as she had challenged her detractors, and again as they had made their way home.

He had always had great sexual appetites, but with Rosalie it was more than lust, more than desire.

She took a section of orange from the tray and squeezed it over his chest. Her eyes glowed with firelight and passion as she leaned down and began to lick the juice away.

"Hmmm, delicious." Her tongue flicked over his nipples.

Passion rode through him on a thundering stallion. She drizzled a trail of chocolate sauce to his waistband, following it with her tongue. The stallion reared on its legs, pawing the air.

"My turn," he said.

She was very still as he removed her clothing piece

by piece. When she was stretched before him on the rug, firelight painting her skin with gold, he took the butterscotch sauce and drizzled it over her nipples. They rose in tight, hard buds. He covered her with his mouth, savoring the sticky-sweet skin, taking her deep into his mouth to get the last of the sauce and the best of Rosalie.

She urged him on with soft cries of pleasure and whispered erotic suggestions. He loved that about her, that such a sweet and gentle woman gave herself up totally to desire.

"You're scrumptious with butterscotch," he murmured, his lips still against her skin.

"Try me with chocolate," she whispered, "and strawberries in exotic places."

The tips of her fingers got the chocolate first, then the tips of her toes. She moaned with pleasure as he sucked the chocolate away.

He shed the rest of his clothes and lay down beside her, drawing her into his embrace. Flames colored them red and gold, warming their already heated bodies. Straining together, hearts pounding and blood racing, they kissed as if they were lovers returning from war.

"The berries," she whispered when they came up for air.

He leaned over her as she lay back on the rug, then took the ripest berries from the bowl.

"Yes," she said later as he went in search of the berries. "Oh, yes . . . yes," she whispered as he closed his mouth over the juiciest one of all.

They played the game until the logs in the fireplace had burned through and turned to smoldering embers. Then, redolent with the scent of oranges and berries and butterscotch, they came together. He rode her fast and hard, just the way she told him to, until at last they lay tangled together, sweaty and sated, beside the empty bowls and the blackened embers.

Betty noticed the difference in Rosalie the minute she walked into the Edge of Paradise late Friday evening.

"Don't tell me that glow came from seeing your boys over Thanksgiving."

"No. I won't tell you that." Smiling, Rosalie got her apron off the hook and tied it around her waist.

Betty drummed her hands on the Formica countertop. "What will you tell me? Not that it's any of my business, mind you. I'm just a curious old bag."

"You're my friend." Rosalie gave Betty a swift hug. "I'm happy, Betty. I know this is not going to last, but while it does, I'm going to enjoy it."

"Of course you won't name names, and I don't expect you to, but if I was going to take a guess, I'd guess he was that man who just walked over to table two looking as if he owned half the world and most of heaven too."

"David!" Rosalie spun around. He was sitting at table 2, gorgeous and sexy, making love to her with his eyes.

She took the coffeepot and went to him.

"Coffee?"

"You."

Their gazes got tangled up, and the temperature rose ten degrees.

"I didn't expect you to come tonight."

"I couldn't stay away."

"If you had told me before I left, you could have come in the car."

"I didn't know it until you pulled out of the driveway."

He reached up, and she reached down. Their hands met, touched, clung.

"I'm glad you came, David."

"So am I."

The hours slid into days, and the days slid into weeks. Rosalie and David were careful not to fall into a routine, not to take each other for granted. They spent each day and each night as if it were their first together, full of surprises and rich with joy.

They had never been happier. Rosalie filled his house with song, and he painted as if he had angels looking over his shoulder.

In their hearts they pretended they could go on forever that way.

The second week of December brought snow to Mississippi. It covered the city with a light blanket, putting a stop to David and Rosalie's walk to the theater. When rehearsal time rolled around, David scraped the windshield on Rosalie's old car, turned the engine on so it could warm up, then drove her through the mushy streets to the theater.

"This is it, cast and crew," the director said after they were all assembled. "Our last week before performance."

Rosalie and David couldn't look at each other. She sat with her hands folded tightly in her lap, and he sat staring straight ahead.

"Starting tomorrow night, we'll begin full dress rehearsals, with makeup."

The director continued his speech by telling the cast and crew how much he appreciated their hard work and what a roaring success the play was going to be.

Rosalie barely heard him. She was thinking about David's leaving. Would he go after the first performance, or would he wait until the last? Would he tell her good-bye, or would he merely walk away? Would he tell her where he was going, or would he just vanish?

Would she die of heartbreak?

"Rosalie . . . Rosalie." The director was calling her name. "Onstage for Act One."

She hurried toward the stage without looking at David. She didn't want him to see her face, didn't want him to see that everything she had told him about wanting a brief interlude to remember was a lie. She wanted him forever. She always had.

Backstage she held her stomach. The Artful Dodger put his hand on her shoulder.

"Are you sick, Rosalie?"

"No. Just butterflies, I guess."

He passed his hand over his forehead. "You gave me a scare. Don't get sick on us now. It's too close to performance time."

"I won't."

If sickness of the heart counted, she was deathly ill. And she was facing the performance of her life—holding back the tears as she let David go.

She waited in the wings for her cue.

They were tense in the car going home. They didn't speak for three blocks. They didn't even touch.

Finally, David broke the silence.

"You were good tonight, Rosalie."

"Thank you."

Two more blocks whizzed by. Rosalie shivered, even in her winter coat with the heater going full blast.

"Are you cold?"

"No."

He didn't offer the comfort of his arm, and she didn't move to his side. What was so natural to them two weeks ago now seemed impossible.

When they reached home, he parked the car, and they sat with the engine running. Usually, when they got back from rehearsals, there was a teasing conversation about his house versus hers.

Tonight they sat staring into the darkness. Rosalie clenched her hands inside her mittens.

"Well, we're home," he finally said, turning off the engine. Without another word he climbed out of the car, then came around to her side and opened her door.

She took his hand and stepped out of the car. In the light of the pale wintry moon they looked at each other.

Suddenly, David reached for her. She rushed into his arms, and they came together in a kiss filled with desperation. The cold wind nipped their noses and bit at their cheeks, but they didn't notice. Wrapped tightly together, they kept on kissing.

When that was no longer enough, he scooped her into his arms and hurried into his house. They were shedding clothes by the time the door closed behind them. Their coats and gloves landed on the den floor. She left her shoes somewhere between the rocking chair and the fireplace and threw her blouse across the desk.

They made it as far as the hallway. She leaned against the wall, her legs weak with desire.

"Now, David. I can't wait."

"Neither can I."

He tore aside restraining clothes, then braced her against the wall. There in the hallway with her legs wrapped around his hips and his hands cupping hers, they tried to die of love.

The fury of their lovemaking drove them until they came to that final act of giving. As the slow, sweet death overtook them, they collapsed against the wall.

Holding him tightly around the waist, she pressed her sweat-dampened cheek against his.

"You'll be leaving in a few days."

The pain in her voice was a knife wound in his heart.

"It's best."

"For you or for me?"

"For both of us."

"I know we said no commitments, and I meant that, David. But I want to know why. Why do you have to leave? You have to live somewhere. Why not here?"

"Because you tempt me to think about the future, Rosalie."

"Is that so bad?"

"There can be no future for me as long as I'm bound to the past."

"By love, David?"

He waited a long time before answering her. Waiting, she died another small death.

He cupped her face with his hands and tipped her face upward. What she saw made her tremble inside.

"By guilt, Rosalie."

Ten

The rest of the week flew by, and they didn't speak of his leaving until opening night.

"Will you leave after the performance?" Rosalie asked.

They were in her house. She was sitting at her dressing table, getting ready to go to the theater.

"I'll stay for them all, Rosalie."

"I want you in the front-row seat where I can see you. You're my good-luck talisman."

David leaned in the doorway, watching her brush her hair. Her right arm was raised, and her head was tilted back. The lamplight shone on the blue veins on the side of her throat and the underside of her arm. He had seen her stretched upon his bed, naked and waiting. He had seen her standing on her kitchen stool, reaching for her cereal. He had seen her through the window, dancing and laughing with her sons.

But the way he loved her most was in this simple pose, rearranging her hair, with her arms stretched above her head and her skin still flushed with loving.

He loved her. The truth came to him suddenly,

unbidden and unwanted. He clenched his jaw, trying to deny it. But with Rosalie sitting in front of him with her pale blue veins pulsing softly underneath her fair skin, denial was impossible.

She turned from the dressing table. "Did you say something, David?"

"No. I didn't say anything." He must have groaned. He had to be careful not to give himself away. They had agreed on an affair, and that's the way he would leave it.

How long had he loved her? For weeks, he was certain. That's probably why he had stopped trying to find a home for Rover. His unconscious mind had known what his conscious mind refused to admit.

"Where will you go, David?" she asked, still facing the mirror.

He didn't meet her eyes; he was afraid she would see the truth.

"I haven't decided." Suddenly, he knew that too. He would go home. Back to Red Bay. Back to pick up the pieces, to get his life together again. Until then, he could never speak love to Rosalie, for he had no idea how long it would take. It wouldn't be fair to give her hope that might be false, to keep her waiting.

Anyhow, she had said nothing about loving him back.

And yet . . .

His gaze strayed to her bed. The covers were still mussed from their recent lovemaking. Over the last three weeks they had told each other in a thousand ways how much they cared.

"Wherever you go, please don't stop painting. You have a beautiful talent."

"Can we make a deal?" He smiled at her, loving her so much, he ached.

"What kind of deal?" Her eyes met his in the mirror.

"I won't stop painting if you won't stop singing."

Slowly, she laid her brush on the table. How could she sing after David was gone? He was her music, the song that sang through her body, her soul, her heart.

"I might stop for a little while . . . but not forever, David."

"Do you promise?"

"I promise." She came to him and wrapped her arms around his waist. "You've given me back my music."

He held her close for what must have been the thousandth time, and yet, knowing he loved her, it felt like the first. Bending down, he pressed his cheek against her soft hair.

They stayed that way for a long time, and then she leaned back in his arms.

"Time to go."

"Break a leg tonight, Rosalie."

"I'll try."

Rosalie stood onstage trying not to see the faces in the audience, save one. David. He was front and center, where he had promised to be.

She thought she would die of love for him in the middle of the stage for all of Tupelo to see. *David*. He would be leaving in two days, and she had never told him she loved him.

There was only one way she could tell him.

Her music cue sounded, and she leaned forward, singing for him, to him—"As Long As He Needs Me." She made all the moves she had rehearsed, but she never took her eyes off him.

When the song was over, the audience rose to its

feet, applauding wildly. Only then did she feel the dampness on her cheeks.

I love you, David.

He met her backstage after the performance.

"You were wonderful. Magnificent. The star of the show."

"You're prejudiced."

"How soon can you get away?"

"Right now."

They slipped out the side door, holding hands. Inside the car she cuddled against his side.

"Tomorrow is Friday. Jack and Jimmy will be coming home for the weekend."

"They're coming to see you in the play."

"Yes."

She didn't have to say any more. David would stay for the final performance on Saturday, but this would be their last night together. The time had come to say good-bye.

He drove slowly, savoring the feel of her head upon his shoulder. It would be the last time.

"My house," she said when he parked the car. "I want to wake up with the pillow on the other side of my bed dented."

He carried her over the threshold like a bride. In her bedroom he unveiled her slowly, as if she were a lost Christmas package that had been found after years of searching. He catalogued every curve, every line of her body. He memorized the texture of her skin, the taste of her lips.

And when he placed her upon the bed, he came to her like a bridegroom, sealing forever his vows of love.

• • •

They awakened early Friday morning, tangled in each other's arms. Rosalie touched David's face.

"Once more, David. And then leave quickly, without saying good-bye."

They said good-bye with their hearts.

The winter sun filtered through Rosalie's curtains, streaking across her linoleum floor, then spread its beams across the Sunday-morning cereal bowls on her kitchen table. She stood at her window.

"You were great in the play, Mom," Jack said.

"Yeah. Terrific. Did you see all of us in the front row giving you that standing ovation. . . . Betty and Jack and me and that neat dude from next door?"

"He has a name, Jimmy. It's David." She held on to the curtain, watching.

Jack and Jimmy looked at each other, their spoons paused in midair.

"You didn't eat your cereal, Mom," Jack said. "Why don't you sit back down and eat?"

"In a little while . . . maybe." She pleated the curtain between her fingers.

Jimmy said a word under his breath. Jack furrowed his brows.

David's back door opened. Rosalie leaned forward propping her elbows on the windowsill. He was carrying two duffel bags, and Rover trotted at his heels.

She held her breath. He stood in his backyard a moment, as if he were taking stock, and then he looked at her window. Their gazes met, held. She squeezed the curtain with both hands.

A taxi pulled into the driveway and honked its horn. Slowly, David turned away. He didn't nod, smile, or acknowledge her in any way.

They could never say good-bye. Their eyes had said it all.

Rosalie stayed at the window until the yellow taxi was far down the street, taking David and his dog to a destination unknown.

He had carried his dog. That was her only hope.

Slowly, she turned back to her sons. "How about chocolate-chip cookies? Or I could make apple pie? Or would you rather have doughnuts?"

Jack came to her and put his arm around her shoulders. "What has he done to make you cry?"

"Me? Crying?" Rosalie put her hands on her face and was surprised to find tears. Furious at herself, she scrubbed them away. "It's called the I'm over thirty-five blues."

"Sit here, Mom." Jimmy pulled out a chair. "Jack and I will make the cookies."

"You are such wonderful sons. What more could a woman want?"

She poured herself a cup of coffee and sat at the table while her sons made cookies. They horsed around, getting more flour on each other than they got in the mixing bowl.

With her hands wrapped around her cup, Rosalie watched them. They were wonderful sons, loving, responsible, hardworking. But she wanted more. The admission, coming so suddenly to her conscious mind, shocked her.

What kind of mother was she? She quickly pushed the old thought pattern aside. A damned good one, that's what kind of mother she was. But being a mother didn't necessarily mean being nothing else at all.

"Jack, Jimmy . . . I need to talk to you."

"Shoot, Mom," said Jimmy, turning with the mixing bowl in his hand.

"I'd like you at the table, please. The cookies can wait."

"This must be serious." Jack straddled the chair across from her.

"It is." Rosalie pushed her coffee cup aside and folded her hands on the kitchen table. Then she drew a deep breath for courage. "I want to make some serious changes in my life, but I can't and won't do it without your cooperation, your permission, even."

She reached across the table for both their hands. "I know how hard you work, and I appreciate that. I don't think I could keep you in school if both of you didn't have part-time jobs."

"It's the least we can do," Jack said.

"How would you feel about taking out a school loan? Not a big one, not for the full amount of your schooling, but just enough to give me money for a voice coach? Somebody here in town, somebody who will tell me whether I have enough talent to keep on trying."

"Hey, Mom, that's great! Jack and I always wondered why you never did anything with your voice."

"You did?" Rosalie was astonished. She supposed she had never considered that children sometimes worried about their parents the same way parents worried about children.

"Yes, we did. You don't have to worry about us, Mom. Jimmy and I are men now. We can take care of ourselves."

"I know you're men, and I'm proud of you." She reached for her hair ribbon. "Lately I've discovered that I want to be proud of myself, as well. Once I dreamed of being an opera singer. Now . . . I know it's late to be starting over, and it's a very long shot, but I want to give it a try."

"We're with you a hundred percent, Mom," Jack said.

"Yeah," Jimmy added. "All the way."

They both came around the table to hug her.

Later that evening, Jack and Jimmy sought out Rosalie at the Edge of Paradise.

"What are you two doing here?" she asked. "I thought you'd be headed back to school by now."

"Shine's going to wait until early in the morning." Jack took her hand and led her back to the kitchen. "Jimmy and I have been talking. We want a family conference."

"With Betty too," Jimmy said. "We've come up with a plan."

"Linda!" Betty yelled to her assistant cook. "Take over here. Got a family emergency that needs my attention." Beaming, she led them to her cubbyhole of an office. "Whatever it is that's got you boys looking like the mouse that belled the cat, I want in on it."

"Here's the plan." Jack took the floor while his mother listened, astonished.

David sat in the Red Bay Police Department, talking to the chief of police, Clyde Downing.

"So, you want your old job back?" Clyde pulled open a fresh bag of corn chips and stuffed one in his mouth. In spite of his habit of nibbling junk food throughout the day, he was hard-muscled and trim.

"If you'll have me."

"You're the best damn cop I ever had. Of course I'll have you." He rammed another handful of chips in his mouth. "That thing with Stephanie. Is it over with?"

"I don't know. I still blame myself. I guess I've got to prove that I can carry out the duties of a police officer without letting emotion cloud my judgment."

"It was her judgment that was clouded, David. She went into that alley alone while you were in the shop next door getting doughnuts and coffee. She broke the rules, and she died for it."

"No. *We* broke the rules, and she died for it. If it hadn't been for what we did . . ." Pausing, David raked his hands through his hair as memories flooded through him. "We had stopped for a break. The kids weren't there when I went into the shop, and then, when I came out, Stephanie was already in the alley. It all happened so fast. I rushed in, but it was too late. They had already knifed her."

"Some officers would have gunned the punks down, but you didn't."

"It was already too late for Stephanie, and they were just kids."

Clyde stood up and offered his hand. "Welcome back, David."

David took a small apartment close enough to walk to the station with his dog trailing at his heels. Rover quickly became the police mascot. A few wags even talked of turning him into a bomb-sniffing dog.

He volunteered for the hardest shifts, numbing his mind to everything except his work. On the job he kept his memories locked tightly away, but in his apartment surrounded by his watercolors of Rosalie, he let them roam free.

At first he suffered. He missed her; he longed for her; he needed her. With only a beer and a dog for companions, he wallowed in his despair.

Even his dog grew tired of listening to him.

"You're right, Rover," David said after a lengthy

recital of woes. "I walked away. And I've got to earn the right to go back."

On Christmas Eve he took up his brushes for the first time since leaving Tupelo. Painting from memory, he did Rosalie at her dressing table, brushing her hair. When he was finished, he went out and bought a tree. It was the first he'd had in many years. Since it was so late, he got the leftovers, the scruffiest one on the lot, but he guessed that would do for starters.

He strung popcorn on the tree, then topped it with a tinfoil star he had fashioned.

"That's the damned ugliest tree I ever saw." His friend and fellow police officer Hubert Franklin had dropped by and was standing inside David's front door, a gift of food in his hand.

"It's my first since I was a kid. I'll eventually get the hang of it."

"Here." Hubert thrust a warm dish into David's hand. "My wife is scared you'll starve to death without her eggplant casserole." He grinned. "I'm taking them around to all the Red Bay PD bachelors."

"Tell her thanks."

"I will, but you need to call her and tell her yourself. She saw you in the grocery store looking at some butterscotch sauce and said you looked like you were pining away and fixing to die."

He had been. Dying of memories.

"June worries too much."

"Yeah . . . well . . . I guess that's why she married me, so she'd have somebody to worry about." Hubert took his hand. "Merry Christmas, David."

"You too, Hubert."

After Hubert left, David poured himself a glass of wine, then sat beside his puny tree looking at his latest painting of Rosalie. She would be celebrating the holiday with her sons and Betty. Did she ever think of him? Ever miss him?

He saluted the portrait with his wineglass. "Merry Christmas, my love."

Betty and Rosalie were putting the final touches on the tree at the café. The last ornament in the box was a pink porcelain rose. Rosalie picked it up and held it to her cheek.

"You miss him, don't you?" Betty asked.

"How did you know I was thinking of David?"

"You had that dreamy look in your eyes."

"I wonder if he's happy, Betty. I wonder if he's celebrating this holiday."

"I wonder if he knows what a good woman he walked out on."

"He didn't walk out. We had an agreement." Rosalie ran her fingers over the porcelain petals of the rose, then tenderly hung it on the tree. "I loved him, Betty. I still do. But even if he were here and even if he loved me, I wouldn't be rushing into another marriage. I have plans." Her eyes began to sparkle. "Big plans."

"You're going to make it, honey." Betty hugged her close. "I know you will."

With each passing day David's guilt over Stephanie's death faded. The pride he took in doing his work well, the encouragement of his fellow officers, and the praise of the chief of police made him feel whole again.

And yet . . . there was one more thing he had to do, one more person he had to see.

He called his ex-wife on the first day of January.

"Gretchen. I need to talk to you."

"You had your chance to talk when we were married. I'm not interested in anything you have to say."

"You have every right to be angry. What I want to do is apologize, and I would prefer to do it in person."

After a long hesitation she agreed to see him. When he hung up the phone, he felt a rush of relief and well-being. He hadn't let her goad him. He hadn't let himself get angry and be drawn into a quarrel. All he felt for her now was a sort of sadness.

Two weeks later he met her at her apartment. She had insisted on both the delay and her home turf. He supposed it made her feel more in control.

He had dressed for the occasion. Although he loathed suits and ties, Gretchen always reacted better to him when he was dressed. "Why do you always insist on looking like a bum?" she used to say. "Other husbands spend their days off in nice-looking khakis and button-down shirts. But you? No. You have to wear those ratty old jeans and tacky old sweat shirts."

He pressed the buzzer. She kept him standing in the cold for five minutes before she came to the door.

"Hello, Gretchen. You look good." She was dressed in yellow, her favorite color.

"I've always thought this color gave my skin a little glow."

He followed her into the living room, thinking of another woman, other skin that didn't need help glowing. *Rosalie.* Desire rushed through him so strong, he had to clench his hands into fists.

"Sit over there, David. Can I get you anything? I have wine chilling."

Wine. He hoped she hadn't thought his visit was to be the resurrection of a dead marriage.

"No thank you. This won't take long."

"Well, why did you bother to come? If you're just going to say your piece, then run out the door, why didn't you say it over the phone?"

He sat down. "I didn't mean it that way, Gretchen." That's the way it had always been with them. Two minutes in each other's company, and he was on the defensive, apologizing for something he hadn't even done.

He supposed that was why he had never apologized to her for Stephanie. Two years earlier he'd figured that he'd done enough apologizing to Gretchen to last a lifetime.

She sat in a chair opposite him and crossed her legs. She'd always had great legs. Two years hadn't changed that.

He studied her face. She was waiting to see his reaction. He kept his expression carefully neutral.

"Gretchen, I came today to tell you I'm sorry. I'm sorry for betraying you. I'm sorry for that one time with Stephanie. . . ."

"Do you have to keep bringing up her name?" Gretchen stood up and began to pace. "I don't want to hear her name again as long as I live. She destroyed my marriage."

"No, Gretchen. *We* destroyed our marriage. It was over long before she came into the picture. I had asked for a divorce. Remember?"

"Do you think that makes what you did all right?"

"At the time I suppose I did. But I was wrong. I broke sacred vows. And for that I'm truly sorry. I should never have hurt you in that way." He went to her and took her hands. "I need your forgiveness, Gretchen."

Anger flashed in her eyes. "You want me to tell you it's all right? That I didn't cry my eyes out for three weeks in a row after you admitted it? That I didn't nearly lose my mind after the divorce?"

"No. I know it wasn't all right. But for that one thing I'm taking all the blame . . . and I'm asking your forgiveness."

"You're not asking that we start over? Try again?"

"No." He squeezed her hands. "You're a beautiful woman, Gretchen, a desirable woman, and I know that someday you'll find someone to love."

"Have you?"

"Yes."

"Before or after the divorce?"

He released her hands and started toward the door. She caught up with him and grabbed his arm.

"I'm sorry, David. Really, I am. I guess I wanted to hurt you."

He turned to her. "Try to be happy, Gretchen. Try to put the past behind you." He kissed her cheek. "That's what I'm doing."

She struggled for composure and won. "Good luck, David," she said, squeezing his arm.

He knew it was the closest she'd ever come to forgiveness. He could accept that.

"You too."

It was two more weeks before David could arrange a short leave of absence from his work. Leaving Rover with Hubert and June Franklin, he boarded the bus for Tupelo.

The house next door to Rosalie's was still vacant. It was a stroke of good fortune he hadn't counted on. The owner was willing to rent it for one week, another stroke of luck.

David paid his week's rent, then took a taxi to Madison Street. When Rosalie's house came into view, he almost shouted for joy. The late afternoon sun slanted on the stained-glass window in her attic room, sending a colored rainbow across her front porch. She would be inside, putting on her pink uniform, getting ready for her evening stint at the café.

As the cab drew closer, he noticed the empty driveway. Was Rosalie's car in the shop? It certainly needed repairs. Or had she gone to work early?

David paid the taxi driver, then entered the creaking old house and stowed his duffel bag. A light came on in Rosalie's house. He hurried to the window.

She was there, moving about her bedroom. He held his breath, watching her. She had done something to her hair. It was shorter, curlier. He felt a moment's regret. He had loved the way she had of reaching to secure her hair in its ribbon.

He leaned closer. Something was not right. Rosalie was too thin. Was she sick?

He had planned to surprise her at the café. To take flowers and champagne, then to escort her home and make slow, sweet love to her upon his bed. But seeing her now, so thin, he knew he couldn't wait. He had to find out what was wrong.

She turned just as he started from the window. David clutched the windowsill until his knuckles were white.

The woman staring at him from across the way was not Rosalie. Frantic, he searched her bedroom. Rosalie's dressing table was not there. Neither was the pink robe she always kept hanging on the closet door.

The woman in the house next door jerked her shade down.

"Fool," David said. "Did you think she would be there always, waiting for you?"

He stood at the window, staring at the house. If he hadn't been so excited about seeing her, he would have noticed the subtle changes. There was a wreath of dried flowers on the back door and a brand-new swing on the front porch. Rosalie could never afford such things, not on her tight budget.

He turned from the window and picked up his coat. There was only one thing left to do, one place left to look. Turning his collar up against the chill, he set out for the Edge of Paradise.

Table 2 was empty. It was too early for the Friday-night crowd. He pulled out his chair and sat down, his eyes searching the room. Rosalie was nowhere in sight.

Big Betty Malone wiped her hands, untied her apron, fluffed up her hair, and left the kitchen for table 2.

"Hello, David. Are you just passing through?"

"I'm glad to see you, Betty." He smiled at her. "No, I'm not just passing through. This is a planned trip."

Betty's expression didn't change. Something was wrong. David felt it.

"Would you like a cup of coffee?"

"I'd like Rosalie."

Betty pulled out a chair and sat down. Premonition prickled the back of his neck.

"Is something wrong, Betty? Has something happened to Rosalie?"

"Rosalie's fine."

"Where is she?"

"Before I tell you that, you've got to answer a few questions."

David's first instinct was to trust Betty. She was Rosalie's closest friend in Tupelo, the nearest thing she had to relatives. Whatever Betty did, she would always have Rosalie's best interests at heart.

He went with his instincts. "If I can," he said.

"Why did you come back?"

"To see Rosalie."

"That's not good enough for me. It's not good enough for Rosalie. Lots of men would like to come and go as they please, spending a few weeks in her bed every time they passed through."

"She told you?"

"She didn't have to tell me. Any fool could see what was going on with the two of you."

"I didn't come back to spend a few weeks in her bed, then leave. I love her, Betty. There were some things in my life I had to deal with before I was free to tell her that."

Betty let out a sigh of relief. "Then I guess it's all right if I tell you."

"Tell me what?"

"I guess she'd want me to."

Alarms began to go off in David's mind. He forced them quiet.

"She's gone. Left Tupelo. Gone off to carve out a career for herself in New York City."

Eleven

Rosalie was living in a small garage apartment in Morristown, New Jersey, working nights in a café owned by Big Betty Malone's brother and commuting days by train into New York to study with a voice coach.

Her life was full and busy. But sometimes at the end of the day when she got back to her empty apartment and pulled off her shoes, she longed to be back home, close to her sons and near enough to Betty so that all she had to do was pick up the phone and say, "Come on over for a game of gin rummy."

But most of all, she missed David. She missed the poetry he used to quote to her late at night after they had made love and were cuddled together under the covers. She missed watching him paint. She missed waking up in the morning and reaching across her bed, knowing he would be there.

It had been a lovely dream while it lasted.

Shaking off her blues, Rosalie threw a coat over her uniform and headed for the café. It was only a three-block walk, but the wind whipped at her coat and hair. February in New Jersey was considerably colder than February in Mississippi.

She was glad to see the neon sign: MURPHY'S PLACE, GOOD FOOD, GOOD ENTERTAINMENT. She slipped in the back door.

"Hi ya, kid. How's it going?" Murphy hollered at her. He was big, burly, and gruff, but likable. Very much like his sister.

"If I had fifty years to study, I might be passable." She hung her coat on the hook and reached for her costume, a simple black dress with beading on the shoulders.

"You're good, kid. Get out there and wow 'em."

"I'll try."

She did two shows at night at Murphy's. Sitting on a tall stool on a small stage in the corner of the café with only a piano for accompaniment, she sang love ballads. Between sets she waited tables.

She walked onstage and leaned over the piano.

"Let's do the *Oliver!* songs tonight, Bill. Key of F."

"Sure thing." Bill was so talented, he made the eighty-eight keys sound like a full band.

Rosalie picked up her microphone and began to sing "As Long As He Needs Me."

Most of the diners kept eating, but a few of them laid down their forks to listen. Rosalie considered that an accomplishment.

She was into the second chorus when David walked through the door. Her voice never faltered, thanks to weeks of training with a demanding voice coach. But her heart almost stopped beating.

She clutched the microphone and looked straight into his riveting blue eyes. Was he still on the run? Was he just passing through?

He sat at a small table in the far corner, never taking his eyes off her. He didn't look as if he were passing through; he had the look of a man who had come to stake a claim.

She sang all her songs to him, for him. *Oh, David, David. Why are you here?*

When she was finished, she hurried from the stage to her small dressing room. She had thirty minutes of privacy, thirty minutes to change into her uniform and pull herself together before she went back into the café. Would David still be there? If she hurried, maybe she could catch him. Did she want to? Could she stand to have her heart broken one more time?

There was a knock on her door. Startled, she clutched her robe around her. No one ever came back there.

"Murphy?" she asked, jerking open the door.

"Happy Valentine's Day, Rosalie." David was standing in the door, holding a single long-stemmed pink rose and a bottle of champagne.

Rosalie's breath caught high in her throat, and she was afraid she might not be able to speak. She clutched the door with one hand and her robe with the other.

"How did you get back here?"

"I flashed my badge." He smiled. "You'd be surprised at how cooperative people are when they deal with an officer of the New York Police Department."

"You're in New York? Since when?"

"Since I couldn't find you in Tupelo . . . May I come in, Rosalie?"

How formal they were, and how sad it felt. Rosalie held the door wide.

"Yes. For a little while. I have to be on the floor in about twenty minutes."

"Murphy said to take as long as you like." He handed her the rose. "For you."

"Thank you." She held it to her cheek, loving the

feel of the soft, velvety petals, loving him for choosing pink. "But it's not Valentine's Day yet."

"It will be next week." He stood close to her, so close, his legs were almost touching hers. She fought for breath. "I've started celebrating holidays, Rosalie."

"Oh, David." Her hand hovered near his face, without touching. If she touched him, she was lost. "I'm happy for you."

Their gazes met, locked. Neither of them could let go. Slowly, David reached for her hand. She couldn't pull away. When he pressed his lips into her palm, her legs threatened to buckle.

"I've missed you so, Rosalie."

His lips were warm and moist and tender. She stole a few more moments of his touch before she pulled away.

"We can't go back, David."

"I don't want to go back. I want to go forward. With you."

She reached for her hair ribbon, only to discover that it wasn't there. She was wearing her hair a new way now, swingy and curved under, more stylish, more sophisticated, something in keeping with her new life. Turning her back to David, she moved away, to the dressing table.

"My life is different now, David. Betty is storing my furniture; the boys have the car. They took school loans so I could come up here and study with a voice coach. This summer they'll live with Betty and help her out at the café."

"I'm proud of you, Rosalie."

"It's what I've always wanted to do. Be an opera singer. My sons are giving me this chance." She picked up her hairbrush—mainly so she would have something in her hand—and began to draw it through her hair. "I can't let them down. I can't let *me* down."

David knelt in front of her and took her hand. "I'm not asking you to give up your dream; I'm asking that you make me a part of it." He pressed her palm to his cheek. "I love you, Rosalie." She started to speak, but he touched her lips with his fingers. "Shh, you don't have to say anything yet. . . . I knew before I left Tupelo. That's why I went back to Red Bay instead of south to Florida."

"You've stopped running?"

"I've stopped running." He smiled at her. "Unless you move to Chicago or London or Paris. I'll run wherever it takes in order not to lose you, Rosalie."

If she had heard those words three months ago, she would still be in Tupelo, Mississippi, working in a law office by day and waiting tables at night, then hurrying home to David's arms, David's bed. She wanted him; she wanted him desperately.

But she wanted more, ever so much more.

"Oh, David," she said, leaning forward, forgetting to hold her robe. It gaped open, exposing the creamy satin chemise she wore underneath, and more, so very much more.

All David's carefully laid plans went up in smoke. He had planned to court her with flowers and champagne, to woo her with old-fashioned declarations of love. Seeing her soft skin shining in the lamplight, he knew he was lost.

Tension crackled the air, and time was suspended. They looked deeply into each other's eyes, and months of separation disappeared; weeks of wanting fell by the wayside.

There was a soft sound, like a kitten mewing, and Rosalie knew she had made it. Slowly, David slid his hands inside her robe, touching her skin with fin-

gers that felt like flame. The need that swept through
her was almost unbearable.

She was in his arms, kneeling with him on the
floor, clutching his shoulders so hard, her nails dug
into his skin.

"I've wanted you every minute of every day since I
left." His mouth was on hers, hard, hungry, demanding.

And it was almost as if he had never gone away.
Pressed so close that his shirt buttons bit into her
breasts, she opened her mouth for the thrust of his
tongue. Clinging to him, weak and wet with desire,
she pulled him down to the rug.

When he was over her, propped on his elbows, his
eyes blazing down into hers, she whispered, "Lock
the door."

She died a small death when he left her there on
the floor. The bolt slid shut with a click.

He was back, hovering over her, devouring her
with his eyes.

"Rosalie?"

"Whatever else happens, David, I have to have
you. This one time." She caught his face and brought
it down to her breasts. "We're safe. No one will come
back here."

He nudged aside the satin and took one creamy
breast in his mouth. Pleasure seared through her,
and her whole body throbbed with wanting. She
arched into his hot, wet caresses, moaning.

With his mouth still on her breast, his hands
roamed down her body, stopping to leave a flaming
imprint in familiar erotic places. Rosalie went wild
under him, shifting so that his hard body was
cradled firmly between her thighs.

He trailed his lips across her throat and back to
her mouth. They kissed as if they had invented it,

kissed until they were panting, kissed until kissing was not enough.

Finally, David broke the contact. His face was tight with passion and the effort of holding back as he gazed down at her.

"I swore never to take you again without telling you I love you." He kissed her forehead, the tip of her nose, her cheek. "I love you, Rosalie. Now and forever."

Her love for him was like a summer garden, lush and beautiful and alive. And yet she couldn't tell him, for hadn't love so often been her downfall? Hadn't it been the thing that killed her dreams?

She was so close now, so very close. She couldn't let love get in the way.

Tightening her hold on him, she pressed him down to her. "Please . . . David, please."

She didn't have to say more. With quick, urgent movements he was inside her. It was a glorious reunion of body and heart and soul that swept them along until they were limp and panting on the floor.

They lay still for a while, with his head resting in the curve of her shoulder and her hands under his shirt, making small, soothing circles on his back.

"David, David," she murmured.

"I'm back, Rosalie. Back to stay."

Shifting, she kissed the side of his neck. His skin was damp and hot.

"Time to go to work," she whispered.

"I'll wait here."

He helped her up, then straightened her satin chemise. Tenderly, he placed a hand on her burning cheek.

He had come to stay. Rosalie picked up her hairbrush and began to untangle her hair. She needed time to think.

He leaned down and braced his hands on the

dressing table, trapping her against his broad chest.

"I want to marry you, Rosalie, and I'm prepared to wait as long as it takes."

"What if I say no?"

"Your body has already said yes. Eventually, your heart will too." He found her eyes in the mirror. "I'm sticking around for your answer."

"And until then?"

"It's up to you, Rosalie. I don't think there's any doubt in your mind that I want you. . . ."

A hot blush colored her cheeks. "No doubt whatsoever."

"But I'm willing to live like a monk, if that's what you want."

"I thought I knew what I wanted . . . until you walked through the door." She felt the hot press of tears clogging her throat. She couldn't cry now; she had to stay focused, strong. "I guess I don't know what I want anymore."

"We both settled for an affair the last time." The muscles in his arms bulged as his hands tightened on the dressing table. His hot body, pressed so close against her back, branded her. "It won't be enough this time, Rosalie."

She didn't answer him, couldn't answer him. He held her with his fierce blue eyes until she finally had to look away.

"I have to go," she said.

"I'll be waiting." He dropped a quick kiss on her bare shoulder, then walked out the door. It clicked shut behind him.

Waiting where? Waiting when? She had been too confused to ask him.

She pressed her hands to her flushed cheeks. If thirty minutes in David's company had her this unfocused, what would seeing him on a daily basis do to her? She had scales to practice, music to learn—in *foreign languages*, for goodness' sake!

Jerking up her uniform, she began to dress. She buttoned her blouse up wrong—twice.

"Dammit," she said. She was going to have to learn to kick furniture. Maybe she could call it artistic temperament and get by with it.

She grinned. She could just hear what Jack and Jimmy would have to say about *that*.

Jack and Jimmy. Oh, my Lord.

She put her head in her hands and groaned. They were sacrificing for her, taking out loans that would have to be paid back.

Resolve filled Rosalie. She couldn't let them down, *wouldn't* let them down. Furthermore, she couldn't let herself down, not this time.

With that decision made, she hurried into the restaurant. She just hoped her resolve would stay strong in the face of David.

"Did your friend find you back there, Rosalie?" Murphy asked as she passed through the kitchen.

"Yes. Thanks. I didn't mean to take so much time."

"You deserve it. The crowds have been great since you started singing here. Anyhow, I thought seeing an old friend might cheer you up."

Murphy threw a slab of ribs on the cutting board and hacked it into serving pieces. "You've looked like you could use it lately, and Betty said if I let you get down in the dumps, she was going to come up here and personally skin me alive."

"You're safe, Murphy. He cheered me up." *And then some.* Her body was still tingling and her skin was still on fire. She hoped nobody would notice.

Tying on her apron and taking up her pad, she went into the restaurant and started waiting tables. She glanced around the room, searching for David. He was nowhere in sight.

She tried to feel relieved about that, but she didn't quite succeed. What she ended up feeling was anxious.

When the time came for her second set, he was still nowhere to be seen. By force of will, she got through her set, then headed back to her dressing room. She half expected to see David waiting for her there.

Her disappointment was almost a tangible thing. She could feel it in the sluggish way she changed her clothes.

"So much for undying devotion," she said, taking her coat off the hook.

It was time to go home.

She stepped outside and pulled her collar up against the chill. It was always colder late at night. Brighter, too, on nights like this.

Rosalie lifted her face to the stars. They were sprinkled like bright confetti across the dark night sky.

"Wish upon a star, Rosalie."

David stepped out of the shadows and stood before her, his eyes blazing into hers.

"I thought you had gone."

"I told you I'd be waiting." He touched her face. "Always, Rosalie."

Her hands trembled as she covered his hand with hers. With his warm fingers on her skin, she felt almost as if she could have it all—David, a career, motherhood, marriage. She kept his hand on her cheek awhile longer, then moved out of his reach.

"Can you get a late train back?"

"No."

She sighed. "Then I suppose you'll have to stay at my apartment tonight."

He moved in and tipped her face up with the back of his hand, studying it by the light of the stark bulb that shone over the door.

"What's this I see? Fear?" His voice was gentle as a caress. "You don't ever have to be afraid of me, Rosalie. I won't do anything you don't want me to do."

"That's just the problem. If you're there, I'll want you to . . ."

"Then I'll find other lodging for the night."

"It's late. This is a small town."

"I can sleep at the station."

"Oh, David." With a smile of resignation, she took his hand. "Come on."

"Where are we going?"

"Home." They set off down the street together, holding hands. "Just this once," she said.

"Your mind is made up, then?"

She stopped under a streetlight beside a maple tree. "Don't you see? I've waited all my life for this. This is my big chance, David. If I don't make it this time, I never will."

"I would never stand in your way, Rosalie. I want to help."

"I know that." She put her hand on his cheek. "Don't you think I do?"

"Then, what?"

She took his hand. "It's cold. Can we finish this conversation inside?"

They walked in silence the rest of the way. Inside her apartment Rosalie brewed hot tea, then curled up on the sofa beside David.

"Having you here, sitting beside me on the sofa, makes all this very hard to say," she told him.

"I'll take heart from that admission."

"Don't. Please don't." She set her cup aside and ran her hands through her hair.

David watched it catch the light of the lamp. Honey and cinnamon. He had always loved her hair, from the very first day he saw her.

"I'm not afraid of you, David, of your lack of support or even of your love. I'm afraid of *me*." She picked up her cup and held it with both hands. It gave her a sense of purpose. "You see, I had plans once, big dreams, and I let my love for Joe Mack sidetrack me. We kept saying, 'Someday we'll have our dreams.' But our love made us comfortable, complacent. We kept putting it off until it was too late."

"You were young then, hardly more than a child."

"And then there was Harry. I *thought* I was in love . . . and I got complacent again. And then I got trapped."

"It would be different with us. We know what we want and where we're going."

"I don't know where I'm going, not yet. And until I do . . ." She set her cup on the coffee table. "I can't see you, David, not for a casual affair, not for a courtship, and certainly not for a marriage."

"I'll accept that . . . for a little while." He reached for her shoulders, drawing her close. "You're the woman I've waited all my life for, Rosalie. The one I thought I would never find. You *are* my life. A miracle." He looked deeply into her eyes, and she thought she was drowning. "I'm not going to let you go."

"Stubborn Irishman," she said.

"Damned right." He released her, and she stood up.

"I'll get your things. You can sleep on the couch."

The couch was old and lumpy. It made his back hurt, but it wasn't the cause of his sleeplessness. Rosalie was. The apartment walls were thin. He had heard her at her bath, then later at her dressing table, dipping into jars and dropping her brush.

Though he had never seen her lose her temper, it sounded as if she might be banging a few things around. He considered that a good sign.

Sighing, he rolled over. The blanket tangled around his legs, leaving his feet sticking out. He just left them there, flapping in the breeze. Might as well add that discomfort to the rest of it—his jaw clenched so hard, his teeth hurt, and his desire so uncomfortably evident, his whole body felt as if it were on a stretching rack.

He rolled over once more, banging his head against the sofa arm. What was the damned thing made of anyhow? Brickbats? He was going to be in great shape tomorrow at the precinct, bleary-eyed and out of sorts.

Well, what had he expected? He had walked away from her without a word. Hadn't even told her where he was going. Did he think he could fly into town and she would come running back to his arms?

He remembered the back room at Murphy's. That didn't count. It had always been like that between them—swift, unbearable need that swept them along in its currents. What he wanted now was commitment, sacred vows that would never be broken. And love.

She had never said she loved him. What if she didn't?

He kicked at his tangled covers and swore. If she wasn't in love with him, he'd just have to see that she fell in love . . . somehow.

"David?"

Her soft voice brought him straight up off the couch. She was standing in her doorway, backlit by a single lamp that burned beside her bed. She was a vamp with a face like an angel and innocence disguised as sin.

He was beyond words. His skin caught fire, and his heart thundered.

"I couldn't sleep." She crossed the room until she was standing beside him. Her diaphanous pink gown brushed against his legs.

"It must be catching. Neither can I." He was surprised he could talk, a man in his condition.

Rosalie bent down and lifted back the tangled covers. "Hold me, David. Just hold me, please."

He opened his arms, and she came into them. They lay back against the lumpy couch, pressed so close together, they felt like one. He smoothed her hair back and rocked her in the tender cradle of his arms, giving his love freely and unconditionally.

"What's wrong, Rosalie?"

"I'm afraid." She pressed her face into the curve between his neck and shoulder. Her breath was warm against his skin. "I'm afraid of making the wrong choices."

"We're all afraid about something, sometime. It's natural."

She squeezed him so hard, he felt the tremble in her arms. "I don't want to lose you, David. . . ."

"You won't. I won't let you."

"And yet . . . I don't want to lose this chance." She sighed. "I don't know what to do. . . ."

"Shhh . . . shhh . . ." He soothed her with his hands, with the gentle rocking motion of his body. "Sleep, Rosalie. Sleep, my love."

They took the same train the next morning. Sitting side by side, with the scenery flying by and the wheels singing their urgent travel song, Rosalie and David didn't talk.

He stared out the window, hoping, and she stared straight ahead, wishing.

At the station he took her hand. "I'll leave you now, Rosalie. I'm going to give you some time."

"You're sweet, David. . . . Thank you."

"You know where to find me if you need me . . . for anything. Any time of day or night. I'll be there for you." He leaned down and brushed a light kiss across her lips. "I love you, Rosalie. Remember that."

"I will."

He turned and walked swiftly away, tall and proud and wonderful. With her hand on her lips, holding on to the lingering warmth of his kiss, she watched him go.

They never said good-bye. Was that because they knew they would be seeing each other again . . . somewhere, sometime?

Rosalie watched until he was out of sight, then hurried into the street to hail a cab. Her voice coach was waiting.

Twelve

Mirella Tagliovini stood by her window, looking down on her private courtyard. One slender hand clung to a silver-handled walking cane, and the other worried at a gold watch pinned to her shirtfront. To the ordinary observer, she might have seemed to be lost in her garden view, but Rosalie was no ordinary observer. She knew that her voice coach was totally alert to everything that happened in the music room.

"Good morning, Rosalie," she said, with her back still turned to the door. "You're five minutes late."

"I'm sorry." She knew better than to make excuses, for they didn't work with Mirella Tagliovini. Instead, she stood on the polished wooden floors in a patch of sunlight, waiting.

Mirella turned around and unexpectedly smiled. "It is of no consequence. You will work hard and make up for lost time." She walked to a velvet-covered Victorian chair and sat down. "Today you will sing Puccini—"*Vogliatemi bene . . . Oh! quanti occhi fisi.*'" She ran her fingers over the watch at her breast. "I've asked Rodolfo to come in and sing with you."

The great love duet from *Madama Butterfly*. Rosalie clenched her hands and hid them in her skirt. How could she sing of love when she had just walked away from David? How could she sing at all when she had just let the music walk out of her life?

"Ready, Rosalie?"

She nodded.

Mirella Tagliovini clapped her hands, and the acclaimed Rodolfo walked through the door. He had sung in London, Rome, and Paris. He had sung with all the great sopranos of the world . . . and now he was going to sing with Rosalie.

She unclenched her fists and forced herself to relax. This is why she had come to New York, why she was risking all her savings, why she was working with Mirella Tagliovini.

"Are you surprised, Rosalie?" her teacher asked.

"Overwhelmed is a better word."

"You want to be great? You work with the best. . . . Now, it is time to begin." Mirella Tagliovini leaned back in her chair and closed her eyes. It was her signal.

All the fullness of Butterfly's heart possessed Rosalie as she beseeched her partner, "Love me with a little love, a childlike love." Her voice soared, blended with his, then took flight again, pouring out the yearnings of her own heart.

When the music ended, Mirella opened her eyes. Rosalie held her breath as her teacher sat perfectly still, staring at them.

Slowly, the old woman left her chair and came to Rosalie. "Tears, my child?" she asked softly, placing her hand on Rosalie's cheek.

"I couldn't help it. I felt the song in my soul."

"My dear . . . don't apologize. I heard the anguish of your heart. It was superb . . . magnificent."

"The pain was real," Rosalie said quietly.

"It is good for an artist to suffer."

Rosalie suffered for days. She tried to drown herself in work, but the harder she pushed, the more she missed David. In desperation she splurged on a long-distance phone call to Betty Malone.

"Rosalie! Is something wrong, honey?"

"How did you know?"

"You don't usually call during the middle of the day."

"Why didn't you tell me he was coming, Betty?"

"He wanted to surprise you. You know what a romantic I am. Been through three husbands and still believe in true love. Ain't it a hoot? It must be the influence of that old country-western song Mickey Gilley sings. You know the one—'True Love Waits.'"

Rosalie gripped the receiver, wondering how long David would wait for her.

"Rosalie . . . are you still there, honey?"

"Yes. I'm here. I know this is silly of me, but I guess I wanted to listen more than I wanted to talk. You always had a way of making me feel that everything was going to be all right . . . even when I knew it wasn't."

"I don't understand what's got you all in a bother. David said he loved you, wanted to marry you. . . ."

"That's just the problem. I can't marry him."

"I'd like to know why in tarnation not? Two's a mighty comforting number. Much better than one. Shoot, I always figured I'd find somebody again one of these days and give it another whirl myself. . . . You haven't changed your mind about him, have you?"

"No. I still love him."

"Then, honey, for goodness' sake, I don't think

you've got a thing in the world to be blue over . . . except maybe you're lonesome for the Edge of Paradise." Betty laughed at herself.

Though she was no closer to a decision than she had been before, Rosalie felt cheered. Betty had always done that for her, cheered her up when it seemed the world was crumbling around her feet.

"Thanks, Betty. I feel better."

"Great. How's the singing coming along?"

"My voice coach says I'll be ready to start auditions in a few months."

"You'll do great, honey. Just think of Big Betty down here pulling for you."

They chatted for a while longer, talking about the boys and the café and the latest doings at the theater.

After she hung up, Rosalie headed for Murphy's Place. She chose the songs from *Carousel* for her first set. As she sang, she searched the crowd for David.

It had been a week since she had last seen him, last touched him, last kissed him. How long would he stay away? Would he grow tired of waiting?

With one leg hooked around the stool, she leaned into the microphone and crooned the beautiful song "If I Loved You." In song she vowed time and again that she would tell her hero she loved him.

When the last note of music died away, she looked out across the restaurant, still searching for David. She had never told him that she loved him. Remembering all the times she could have, *should* have, she was extraordinarily sad.

"Expecting someone, Rosalie?" the pianist asked.

"No, Bill. I guess not."

Back in her dressing room, she pulled off her costume and sat at her dressing table. A single pink rose, drooping and dying, stood in a bud vase on the edge of the table.

"Happy Valentine's Day," David had said.

She lifted the rose carefully out of the water, dried the stem with a tissue, then laid it on the table. One perfect rose. David had used it to mark all their significant occasions together.

"I'm celebrating holidays now." His eyes had been shining when he'd said that.

Tomorrow would be Valentine's Day. A perfect day to celebrate love.

Without any warning, the blues that had plagued her for days vanished. Smiling, she leaned over and touched the rose.

"Happy Valentine's Day, my love," she whispered.

David sat at his desk in the stationhouse, cleaning up some last-minute paperwork.

"Hey, Kelly. You got big plans for tonight?"

Wayne Maycomb, the precinct's resident Romeo, looked up from his work. He was big, burly, and friendly, and he made David's transition to the NYPD an easy one.

"Nothing except a good hot soak in the tub."

"With a woman, I hope."

"Not a chance."

"You need major rehabilitation, man." Wayne shrugged into his New York Yankees jacket. "How about coming with me tonight? I know at least three women who would be glad to put a smirk on that ugly mug of yours."

"Thanks, but not tonight, Wayne."

Wayne ran a pocket comb through his mop of unruly red hair. "Then I'll catch you later, pal. Happy Valentine's Day."

"Yeah. Same to you."

David shrugged into his jacket and turned his collar up. He rammed his hands into his pockets and walked out into the street. Going home alone. It wasn't what he expected to be doing.

He passed a drugstore on the way to his apartment and stopped to look in the window. Red hearts and boxes of candy tied with red ribbon filled the window, reduced. LOVE AT HALF PRICE, the sign said.

David walked on. He would take love at any price. Rosalie's love. How much longer could he endure before he bulldozed his way into her life again?

He kicked at an empty beer can in the street, then stooped to pick it up and throw it into the nearest garbage. He had told her he would give her time, and that's what he was going to do. Even if it killed him.

A huge poster for Mystic Persian Potion decorated the window of a sleazy store offering aphrodisiacs, guaranteed to work. The lovers on the poster were in a clinch.

David hurried on by, jealous of painted people on a cardboard poster. He was going to do a hundred sit-ups when he got home, and then get in a cold shower.

"Dammitall," he muttered when a cat streaked out of the alley by his building and tangled between his feet. It was a big yellow tom. "Go on, cat. Go get yourself a girl. Everybody else has."

He went into the lobby of his apartment building. The long climb up the stairs did nothing to improve his mood. He rattled the key in his ill-fitting lock, then pushed open his door.

Instantly, he was alert. Someone was in his apartment. He could feel it, smell it. Moving quietly, he reached inside his jacket to his shoulder holster.

The faint scent of roses wafted over him.

"Happy Valentine's Day, David." Rosalie stepped out of the shadows and flicked on a lamp. "Surprise." Smiling, she held her arms wide.

In two strides he was across the room, wrapping

her in his arms, hugging her so close, she feared for her ribs.

"David." She laughed, leaning back to look up at him. "You don't have to hold on so tight. I'm not going anywhere."

"How did you get up here?" he asked, leading her to the sofa.

"By lying. I told the landlord I was your sister, and I had come all the way from Alabama with news I knew you'd want to hear."

He leaned just far enough back so he could look into her eyes. What he saw there made him dare to hope. "And what is this news, Rosalie?"

Tenderly, she traced his face with her hands, starting with his eyebrows and ending with his lips. "That I love you, David. That I loved you in Tupelo, and I loved you in New Jersey, and I love you in New York."

Smiling, she pressed her lips to his for a kiss that was so sweet, he thought he heard angels singing.

"You're my last and my best love, David."

There was so much he wanted to say, so much he wanted to ask. But she was in his arms, her eyes gleaming, her lips beckoning, and already his skin was on fire.

He pulled her so close, he could see her soul through the shining center of her eyes.

"You told me you've started celebrating holidays," she whispered, her mouth only inches from his.

"Because of you." He ran one finger along the moist inner lining of her lower lip.

"I think it's past time to celebrate Valentine's Day, don't you?" She pulled his shirt out of his pants and ran her hands over his chest.

"Do you have anything in mind?"

"This . . ." she said, pressing her lips into the

hollow of his neck. "And this . . ." She reached for his belt buckle.

"Say it again, Rosalie," David told her as he slowly peeled away her clothes.

"Happy Valentine's Day."

"No. The other." He lowered her to the sofa, and she smiled at him, honey and cream, fire and smoke.

"I love you, David." She reached for him, and he came to her, sliding home where he belonged. "I love you . . . I love you," she chanted softly, keeping time to the slow, bluesy rhythm of their loving.

A week of separation had made them hungry, and they were soon racing toward that final destination, their voices lifted in triumph when they reached the goal.

He shifted so that they were facing each other on the narrow couch.

"Marry me, Rosalie."

"I didn't come here tonight to tell you I would. I merely came to say 'I love you.'" She kissed the side of his jaw, then found the scar on his back. Tenderly, she traced its jagged line.

"Are you afraid of my profession, Rosalie? Afraid the next knife will find my heart?"

"I was afraid of everything . . . until we came together again on this lumpy sofa."

He laughed. "We can do something about that." Scooping her up, he carried her into his bedroom, finding the way in the dark. In the glow of neon from the pool hall next door, he bent over her and searched her face.

"I won't settle for an affair this time, Rosalie."

"Are you asking me to leave?" she whispered, cupping his face and pulling it down to hers.

He took her lips in a kiss that seared their souls. "I'm asking you to stay . . . forever."

"Only tonight, David."

"And tomorrow night?"

"I'll come again after my lesson, before I take the train back to New Jersey."

"And the night after that?"

Seeing how complicated it would all be, she bit her lip. "I don't know. Maybe you can come to my place."

"My place or yours. Is that what you want, Rosalie?"

She laced her hands into his hair and pulled his head down to her breasts. "I want you, David."

As always with them, passion burst quickly into full flame. David took her deep into his mouth, knowing that for now that's all he had of Rosalie, her part-time love.

With the blue neon from next door veiling her skin in mystery, he savored her, slowly and completely, finding every curve, every hollow, that he loved so dearly. He branded the soft, satiny skin from her breasts all the way down to the juncture of her thighs.

"Love me, love me, David," she whispered, offering herself to him—the musk and honey of her body, the tender music of her soul.

He took her, all of her. With her fingernails dug into the sheet, she urged him on with desperate whispers. Her world splintered into bright pieces, then came together in one burning star, and that star was David. He burned in her and through her and around her, far into the night.

And when the first pale rays of morning washed over the windowsill, she fell asleep, exhausted, in his arms.

David cradled her, watching her sleep. She had come to him. After one agonizing week of waiting and wondering, he had found her in his apartment, willing to be in his arms.

It wasn't all he wanted, but it was a start. He held

her until the sun sent a shaft of light over his covers. He didn't have to look at the clock to know it was time to go.

He reached for the tangled sheet and tenderly pulled it over her. Then he set the clock so she wouldn't miss her lessons and headed for the station.

"You look like hell," Wayne Maycomb said. "Rough night?"

David smiled.

"Well, go ahead. Keep secrets after I offered to share," Wayne teased good-naturedly.

"She's special, Wayne. And if I'm lucky, she'll be wearing my ring one of these days."

Wayne groaned. "Not the old ball and chain. I thought you were a better man than that. An artist, for crying out loud."

"Painting is just something I do."

"My sister loved that watercolor of yours I gave her for her birthday. Said she was going to show it to a friend of hers who has a gallery."

"I appreciate that. Tell her I said so."

"If I know Becky, she'll be down here thanking you. She considers herself a patron of the arts, and she loves discovering new talent."

"I don't know that I'm 'new talent.' I'm just a police officer who loves to paint."

"Don't tell that to Becky. Tell her you live and breathe for art. Tell her your soul would shrivel and die without it. That's the kind of thing patrons love to hear from artists."

The only thing David would shrivel and die from was losing Rosalie. But he didn't tell Wayne that. He merely went about doing his duties as an officer of the law.

• • •

Although she had had very little sleep in David's apartment, Rosalie's voice didn't suffer. In fact, she had never had a better lesson.

"You are competing with the angels today, Rosalie," Mirella said, smiling her approval.

"It's because of David." She spoke his name out of the joy that overflowed her heart, but she instantly saw her mistake.

"David?" Mirella frowned. "Who is this David?"

"A good friend . . ." she said, seeking to avoid further discussion. Then, feeling disloyal to David, she added, "Actually, he's more than a good friend. He's the man I love."

"Ahhh . . . love." Mirella walked to her window and stood gazing at her courtyard.

Rosalie waited, wondering what would come next. Was she to be dismissed because she dared to love?

Mirella's eyes glittered as hard as the diamonds at her throat and on her fingers when she turned back to Rosalie.

"I cannot tell you how to live your private life. Would that I could!" She threw her hands up in one of her dramatic gestures. "But I will tell you this," she said, tapping her cane on the floor for emphasis. "Let no man come between you and your art, Rosalie. If you do, you are courting failure."

Later that evening Rosalie thought of Mirella's advice as she let herself into David's apartment with the spare key. Joe Mack had come between her and her art. Not deliberately, of course. But being in love and having the twins to care for had taken priority over everything else, including an operatic career.

She paced David's small apartment. Was she capable of handling love and the demands of launching a singing career at the same time? While she was working so hard to establish herself in the world of opera, she would be a part-time wife at best. Would that be fair to David?

Maybe it would be easier for both of them if she just left. In time they would forget the high, bright passion they felt for each other. In time their love would fade. He was an artist; she was a singer. Pain could be metamorphosed into beauty in art.

If she hurried, she might catch the next train back to New Jersey. She was reaching for her purse when the door opened.

David stood just inside the doorway, piercing her with his fierce blue eyes. He looked tired.

"Were you leaving me, Rosalie?" he asked, looking at the purse in her hand.

"Yes."

They stood facing each other across the room. The pain in his eyes flayed her heart. Her hands tightened on her purse, and her tongue flicked over her lips.

David didn't move. He merely stood there, quiet and magnificent, waiting for her.

Her purse slid to the floor as she ran across the room and launched herself into his arms.

"David, David," she whispered, pressing her face against his chest. "I'm so selfish."

"You're just scared." He cradled her in his arms and pressed his lips to her hair.

"Hold me, please. Don't let go."

He held her, gentling her with his hands, soothing her with soft whispers of love. Sighing with contentment, she burrowed close, feeling protected and comforted and cherished.

As always with them, the hot press of passion soon would not be denied. He opened his buttons and ran her hand inside his shirt. He pushed her skirt up and spread his hands upon her warm skin. Urgently, she moved against his fingers, and they fell victim to their desires.

"Rosalie." He spoke her name with fervor, as if the very sound of it was too erotic to bear.

"Take me, David," she whispered. "Now."

In the hard, bright stillness of that room he took her quickly, bracing her against the wall. They loved with desperation and fierceness, as if they feared that this time would be their last.

And when it was all over, David quietly lowered her to her feet and rearranged her clothes. Rosalie stood very still, letting him take care of her.

"I love you, David," she whispered. "Please don't ever doubt that."

"I love you, Rosalie." He traced her cheeks with his fingertips. "I could paint this face in my sleep. These cheekbones . . . this skin . . . these lips."

Rosalie held her breath, trying to stop the minutes that were hurrying by. David pushed back her damp hair, then bent to kiss her forehead. She felt tears gathering at the back of her throat.

"The noblest part of loving is letting go." He got her purse off the floor and placed it in her hand, curving her fingers around the handle, then holding on. "I'll take you to your train."

"Yes."

She had her sets to do at Murphy's Place. The rest of the world didn't stop for love.

They were silent as they made their way to the train station. And when the gleaming tracks came into sight, and the hulking mass of steel that would take her back to New Jersey, she squeezed his hand. It seemed to her that she and David were always going in different directions, always parting without saying good-bye.

This time was no different. He put her on the train with a light kiss on the cheek, then stood by the tracks watching her leave. She pressed her face to the window and kept it there until he was a speck in the distance.

"Good-bye, my love," she whispered.

That evening, sitting on her solitary stool at Murphy's Place, she sang "As Time Goes By." Tears wet her eyes and rolled down her cheeks as she remembered the final scene of *Casablanca*, Bogart saying good-bye to Bergman.

She couldn't have it all. Not this way. Two days of taking late trains to New Jersey proved that. She would be exhausted. And what about David? She couldn't let him be the one to take the late trains—or the early morning ones, depending on whether he stayed the night. His work was too dangerous. What if another drug-crazed kid came out of the alley while David was mentally and physically drained? He would be dead. And it would be her fault.

Love wasn't supposed to kill.

After her first set, Murphy stopped her on the way to the dressing room.

"Something bothering you, Rosalie?"

"Yes, but I'll try not to let it affect my work."

"It's not that. You're doing a fine job." He put his arm around her shoulders and led her to a quiet spot in the kitchen. "Time for tea and sympathy, honey," he said, pressing a cup of hot tea into her hand.

"Thanks, Murphy. You're a friend."

"Heck, I've grown about as attached to you as my sister has." They sipped tea in silence a while, then he patted her hand. "Just remember this, honey. Ain't nothing wrong that a little old-fashioned determination can't fix."

Old-fashioned determination. Rosalie thought about Murphy's advice the rest of the night and all the way into New York the next morning.

She looked out the window of the train at the countryside rolling by. Until a few months ago all of it had been unfamiliar to her, almost a foreign land. She had been born southern, brought up southern, and lived southern. All her life had been spent with the safe, the familiar . . . until David had given her the old-fashioned determination to reach out for more. He had given her back her music, her dreams, and her desire to reach for them. He had opened another world to her, a world filled with brilliant explosions of beauty and passion.

But most of all he had given her an explosion of self, a fierce, startling discovery that she was a person with potential, a woman of possibilities. Her life would be exactly what she made it. That, and no more.

When the train pulled into the station, she was the first one to get off. The nearest phone booth was only a few minutes away. She headed toward it, walking with a new confidence. With her hands tight on her purse, she pushed open the door and slid into the booth.

"This is Rosalie Brown," she said after Mirella Tagliovini picked up the phone. "Could we possibly reschedule my lesson today? I have something very important that I have to take care of."

David was in the records room, going through old files, when Wayne stuck his head in the door.

"Hey, Kelly. There's someone to see you."

"Can you take care of it, Wayne? I'm covered up back here."

"I'd handle it personally if I was you."

"Yeah? What's it all about?"

"Why don't you let the lady tell you herself?" Grinning, Wayne stepped aside.

Rosalie stood in the doorway, as bright and fresh as the morning. Slowly, David laid the records aside.

"How about if I leave you two alone? I'll even shut the door." Wayne gave the thumbs-up sign before he left the room, closing the door behind him.

"Rosalie," said David, being careful not to let the wild hope that roared like a river through his soul show in his voice.

"David." She smiled at him, almost shyly. Then she shrugged off her coat and lifted her arms to rearrange her hair, as if the train ride in the closed car from New Jersey had mussed the shining strands.

Seeing the pulse of pale blue veins under skin, he fell in love with her all over again.

"Is something wrong, Rosalie?"

"No. Everything is . . . almost perfect."

He dared not touch her, dared not fan that flame that would burn so quickly out of control. With great force of will, he stayed where he was, keeping the filing cabinet between him and the object of his obsession.

"Can I get you some coffee?" he asked. "Tea?" She shook her head. "Can I do anything for you?"

"When we were in Tupelo, life seemed so simple. I would go to the Edge of Paradise while you waited at home, painting one of your beautiful pictures, or building one of your birdhouses." She took a step toward him, then stopped. "Every day I knew that you would be waiting for me, that I would go to sleep at night with you at my side and I would wake up in the morning with your head denting the pillow next to mine."

His heart leaped with joy, but he bade it wait. *Not yet*, he said to himself. *Don't push her.*

"I want it back, David. All of it. Not in Tupelo, but here, in New York. I want to kiss you good-bye in the morning before I go to lessons, and I want to kiss you hello at night when you come home."

"Rosalie . . ."

He started toward her, and she started toward him. They met halfway across the room. Locking hands, they gazed at each other.

"Take me back, David. Take me back to the edge of paradise."

"Not this time, Rosalie." He bent to kiss her lips. "This time we're going all the way.

Epilogue

Seven Years Later

ROSALIE KELLY DEBUTS AT THE MET, the headlines said.

Setting the newspaper aside, Big Betty wiped a her eyes, then pulled a handkerchief out of her apron and blew her nose.

"Silly, sentimental old fool," she said.

"Now, honey, that's not true." Robert Larkin, the best cook in Tupelo, left the burgers sizzling on the range and came to put his arms around her. "I won' have my bride talking that way about herself."

"We've been married two years, you smooth- talking old fox."

He grinned and kissed her soundly on the lips never mind that the new waitress was gawking around the door.

"That's why you married me."

Big Betty grinned. "You keep that up, and I'll show you why I married you."

Laughing, she picked up the paper once more. "Listen to this. 'Local woman makes good. Newcomer Rosalie Kelly proved herself worthy to join the roster of outstanding lyric/coloratura sopranos when she debuted at the Metropolitan Opera in *The Barber of Seville*. As Rosina, she sparkled with vixenish charm and *fioritura* brilliance, especially in the lesson scene.'" Grinning, she winked at her husband. "That's my Rosalie."

"They left out how she sparkled with beauty," Robert said. "Sitting there on them reserved seats, I was as proud of her as if she had been my own."

"Wait, wait. Listen to this. 'Patrons of the arts will also know Rosalie Kelly as wife of Captain David Kelly, the artist/police officer whose work is gaining attention throughout the United States.'" Betty wiped another tear. "If I don't hush this bawling, I won't be fit to welcome the special guests."

The cowbell clattered in the old café, and the first special guest walked through the door. Jack Westmoreland came striding in, one arm around his fiancée, Maribeth Moore, and the other held wide for Big Betty.

"Jack!" she screamed, running to him. "How's the best-looking future veterinarian in the state doing?"

"Can't complain." Jack grinned. "And if I did, Maribeth would nail my hide to the barn door."

"You're darned right I would." She smiled at him, showing her dimples.

The cowbell clattered once more, and Jim Westmoreland strolled in, looking grand and handsome in his navy uniform.

Robert was the one who greeted him first, calling him the "best damned pilot in the whole U.S. of A."

Big Betty brought out the cookies; her husband brought out the milk, and they all sat around talking old times, waiting for the other special guests to arrive.

"Don't you think these boys might be getting a little old for milk and cookies, honey?" Robert asked.

"Not as long as I'm living. They're still my babies."

There was a commotion at the door. Big Betty put her hand over her heart and watched Rosalie Kelly enter the old café. Time and success and love had heightened her beauty, deepened her spirit.

"Welcome back, honey." Betty ran to her, holding her arms wide. "Welcome back to the Edge of Paradise."

Rosalie held her close, her dearest and best friend—neither time nor distance could change that. Then she reached back and caught her husband's hand. "Thanks to David, I never left."

He put his free arm around his wife's waist and smiled down into her eyes.

"What about me, Mommy? What about me?" The little dark-haired girl in David's other arm chanted, regarding them all with her bright blue eyes.

"You, too, my darling," she said to her daughter. "You, too."

Much later that evening, with her sons bedded down on sleeping bags in Betty and Robert's sprawling country house, and her future daughter-in-law and five-year-old daughter sleeping in spare rooms down the hall, Rosalie sat at the dressing table, tying a ribbon in her hair.

David leaned against the bedpost, watching her.

"I love watching you do that," he said.

"I'm getting too old for ribbons."

"Never."

Their eyes met in the mirror, and she smiled at him.

"I had given up ribbons, you know," she teased him.

"Only in public."

"Remember when I put that first ribbon in my hair again. . . ." Her eyes shone with memories.

He left his watch at the bedpost, and bending down, embraced her from behind. "I did this," he said, cupping her breasts.

Her reaction was clearly visible through the sheer lace bodice of her gown.

"And I did that," she said, laughing at her instant reaction to him.

"I believe I'm getting old. You'll have to show me what we did next."

She turned and stood up in his arms. "What we did next was create our little miracle, Ariel."

He kissed the side of her throat where the soft blue veins pulsed, then nudged aside her straps.

"What we always do together is create a miracle, Rosalie," he whispered, right before he took her deep into his mouth.

She wound her hands into his hair, holding him close. "Oh, yes, David. Yes."

In the moonlight the white canopied bed beckoned.

THE EDITOR'S CORNER

There are certain stories we all know and love, whether they're fairy tales, classic novels, or unforgettable plays. We treasure them for the way they touch our heart and soul, make us laugh or cry—or both—and next month LOVESWEPT presents you with a bounty of **TREASURED TALES**, six wonderful romances inspired by beloved stories. With special messages from the authors and gorgeous covers featuring black-and-white photographs that reflect the timelessness of these stories, **TREASURED TALES** are worth a king's ransom!

Starting the lineup is Helen Mittermeyer with **'TWAS THE NIGHT,** LOVESWEPT #588, a stirring version of **BEAUTY AND THE BEAST**. It was on Christmas Eve that Rafe Brockman and Cassie Nordstrom first met, but then they parted as enemies. Now, years later, fate brings them together again on Christmas Eve, and they learn that the gift of love is the true Christmas miracle. A heartwarming story from one of the genre's most popular authors.

In **THE PRINCESS AND THE PEA,** LOVESWEPT #589, Fayrene Preston gives her heroine something more intriguing—and gorgeous—to deal with than a troublesome legume. Though Cameron Tate is the perfect hunk to star in a jeans commercial, all Melisande Lanier wants from him is his bed. But Cameron will sell only if workaholic Mel slows down long enough to fall in love with him. Fayrene's winning charm makes this enchanting story shine.

Like Sydney Carton in Charles Dickens's *A Tale of Two Cities,* Nick Atwell is a rebel with a taste for trouble, but his **RENEGADE WAYS,** LOVESWEPT #590 by Terry

Lawrence, can't dissuade Connie Hennessy from believing the handsome diplomat might be just the hero she needs. And she quickly lets Nick know she's willing to barter heated kisses for Nick's help in a perilous mission. Terry really lets the sparks fly between these two characters.

With **NIGHT DREAMS,** LOVESWEPT #591, Sandra Chastain gives us a hero as unforgettable as the Phantom from *The Phantom of the Opera*. No one knows the truth behind the legend of Jonathan Dream, the playboy who'd vanished after building an empire. But when Shannon Summers is taken to his castle to help his disabled daughter, she learns of his scars and his secrets—and burns with the wildfire of his desire. Sandra tells this story with stunning force.

Snow White was contented living with the seven dwarfs, but in **THE FAIREST OF THEM ALL** by Leanne Banks, LOVESWEPT #592, Carly Pendleton would like nothing better than for her seven loving, but overbearing brothers to let her have her own life. Longtime friend Russ Bradford agrees, especially since he has plans to claim her for his own and to taste the sweetness of her ruby-red lips. Leanne delivers a wonderfully entertaining read.

Peggy Webb will light up your day with **DARK FIRE,** LOVESWEPT #593. Although Sid Granger isn't as short on looks as Cyrano de Bergerac, he doesn't dare court the beautiful Rose Anne Jones because he thinks he can never match her perfection. Instead he agrees to woo her for a friend, but the thought of her in another man's arms sends the fighter pilot soaring to her side. Peggy has once again created an irresistible, sensuous romance.

On sale this month are four fabulous FANFARE titles. From *New York Times* bestselling author Amanda Quick comes **RECKLESS,** a tale of a tarnished knight, a daring maiden, and a sweet, searing, storybook love. When

Phoebe Layton needs help to carry out a quest, she can imagine no one more suited to the job than Gabriel Banner. But the Earl of Wylde has a quest of his own in mind: to possess Phoebe, heart and soul.

The Delaneys are here with **THE DELANEY CHRIST-MAS CAROL!** For this long-awaited addition to this enduring family's saga, Kay Hooper, Iris Johansen, and Fayrene Preston teamed up once again, and now we're thrilled to give you three tales of three generations of Delaneys in love and of the changing face of Christmas—past, present, and future. Enjoy our special holiday offer to you.

If you missed Tami Hoag's novel **SARAH'S SIN** the first time around, you can pick up a copy now and discover a warm, moving story of two cultures in conflict and two hearts in love. Matt Thorne is every fantasy Sarah Troyer has ever had. And though there's a high price to pay for giving herself to one outside the Amish ways, Sarah dares to allow herself a brief, secret adventure in the arms of a forbidden man.

Maureen Reynolds has been described by *Romantic Times* as "a very HOT writer," and the tempestuous historical romance **SMOKE EYES** will show you why. Katherine Flynn has worked hard to overcome the double prejudice she faced as a woman and an Arapaho half-breed, but she can't win against the power of desire when Zach Fletcher abruptly returns to her life.

Also on sale this month in the Doubleday hardcover edition is **CONFIDENCES** by Penny Hayden. In the tradition of Danielle Steel, **CONFIDENCES** is a deeply moving novel about four "thirty-something" mothers and a long-held secret that could save the life of a seventeen-year-old boy.

Well, folks, it's around that time of year when people usually take stock of what they've accomplished and look forward to what's ahead. And one of the things we've been taking stock of is **THE EDITOR'S CORNER**. It's been a continuing feature in LOVESWEPT books since LOVESWEPT #1 was published. That makes almost ten years' worth of previews, and we wonder if it's still something you look forward to every month, or if there's something else you'd like to see perhaps. Let us know; we'd love to hear your opinions and/or suggestions.

Happy reading!

With warmest wishes,

Nita Taublib
Associate Publisher
LOVESWEPT and FANFARE

RECKLESS
by Amanda Quick
the *New York Times* bestselling author of
RAVISHED and SCANDAL

From a crumbling fairy–tale castle on the stormy Sussex coast to a dazzling, dizzying masquerade ball comes an enchanting tale of a tarnished knight, a daring maiden, and a sweet, searing, storybook love. . . .

At sixteen Phoebe Layton had imagined that Gabriel Banner was a brave and valiant knight, a noble–hearted hero born to rescue ladies in distress. Which was why, eight years later, when she desperately needed help to carry out a vital quest, she could think of no one more suited to the job than Gabriel.

But when she lures her shining knight to a lonely midnight rendezvous, Phoebe finds herself sparring with a dangerously desirable man who is nothing like the hero of her dreams, and when he sweeps her into a torrid—and blatantly unchivalrous—embrace, she can't help but fear that she's made a dreadful mistake. It's a kiss that will seal Phoebe's fate. For now the exciting Earl of Wylde has a quest of his own: to possess the most intriguing, impulsive, outrageous female he has ever met . . . even if he has to slay a dragon to do it.

THE DELANEY CHRISTMAS CAROL
by Kay Hooper, Iris Johansen, and Fayrene Preston

**The Delaney Dynasty continues with three tales
of Christmas—Past, Present, and Future**

CHRISTMAS PAST
by Iris Johansen

*From the moment he first laid eyes on her, Kevin Delaney felt a
curious attraction for the rag-clad Gypsy beauty rummaging through
the attic of his ranch at Killara. He didn't believe for a moment her
talk of magic mirrors and second sight, but something about Zara St.
Cloud stirred his blood. Now, as Christmas draws near, a touch leads
to a kiss and a gift of burning passion as the Gypsy and the cowboy
discover the sensual magic a man and a woman can make in each
other's arms.*

CHRISTMAS PRESENT
by Fayrene Preston

*Bria Delaney had been looking for Christmas ornaments in her
mother's attic when she saw him in the mirror for the first time—a
stunningly handsome man with sky-blue eyes and red-gold hair. She
had almost convinced herself he was only a dream when Kells Braxton
arrived at Killara. Bria saw romance in their future as her mirror
fogged with steamy kisses and late-night caresses. Soon shadow
would turn to flesh and dreams to real-life passion as the rugged
Australian stepped from her looking glass to lead them both to a
holiday wonderland of sensuous pleasure.*

CHRISTMAS FUTURE
by Kay Hooper

As the last of the Delaney men, Brett returned to Killara this Christmastime only to find it in the capable hands of his father's young and beautiful widow. Yet the closer he got to Cassie, the more Brett realized that the embers of their old love still burned and that all it would take was a look, a kiss, a caress to turn their dormant passion into an inferno. Could their love for each other redeem the past—and save Killara for a new generation of Delaneys?

The three endearing stories of The Delaney Christmas Carol *are unified by a magical mirror. The following excerpt from the book's foreword gives us a glimpse into the history of that enchanting glass.*

Like many stories surrounding the Delaney family, the truth of the mirror was somewhat clouded by conflicting tales. That wasn't unusual, particularly given Shamus Delaney's habit of freely embellishing his family's history, but it did sometimes cause problems for succeeding generations.

Even the most likely explanation for how the Delaney family came to have the mirror was vague, yet colorful. Stripped of all but the barest bones of the story, however, it seems that in his youth in Ireland, Shamus performed some service—about which he was uncharacteristically silent, even in his private journal—for a mysterious tribe of Gypsies. In return, a Gypsy artisan carved a lovely and elaborate frame from bogwood for an oval mirror of exceptional clarity.

Was the frame so special, or the mirror itself? In all the years afterward, no one was prepared to guess. Nor would any Delaney have dared to separate the dark bogwood from the brilliant perfection of the mirror in order to know for sure. For most, that question hardly mattered, because the undeniable fact was that the mirror was far more than glass and wood.

It was a window that offered brief glimpses into the past, present, and future of the Delaney family. But it was a capricious thing. The mirror revealed tragedy as often as triumph and refused to be mastered even by the willful Delaneys. Only some Delaneys saw anything other than their own reflections, and few indeed saw what they wanted to see even when the mirror opened its window into time.

Many of his descendants were divided on whether Shamus knew the true nature of the Gypsies' gift. Some said that he accepted the mirror and stumbled on the truth later, while others were certain that the Gypsies themselves had explained in language fanciful enough to satisfy even the most romantic the true nature of their gift when it was given.

Whatever actually happened during that presentation, time revealed the truth of the mirror. And no doubt there were many Delaneys in the years that followed who believed it was a window best left shuttered, because it wasn't wise for mortal eyes to gaze into the future.

Still, not even the Delaneys who might have wanted to, dared to destroy the mirror. They might well put it away, but it became as much a part of Delaney heritage as the bogwood clock. However, as things put out of sight sometimes fade out of mind, the mirror was either deliberately or accidentally forgotten by the family at various times through the years. Tucked away in an attic or shoved back into a dark corner, it waited patiently to be discovered or rediscovered.

Bits of its history were lost, for a time or forever. Whole generations of the family lived without knowing anything at all about the mirror. But then a curious explorer would find it again and become intrigued. It would be dusted off and polished and brought forth to be exclaimed over.

It possessed its own sense of timing. It always seemed to reappear in the family at critical moments. And, oddly, it favored holidays, particularly Christmas—perhaps because of the holly carved so intricately into its frame, or perhaps simply because Christmas was innately a magical time. In any case, the holiday seemed a perfect time to hang so lovely a thing in a room or hallway of Killara.

And who could resist a glance into a mirror of such exceptional clarity? Few. Most saw only their own reflection, but some saw more.

SARAH'S SIN
by Tami Hoag

"A master of the genre."
—*Publisher's Weekly*

From Tami Hoag, award-winning author of *Lucky's Lady* and *Still Waters*, comes ONE OF HER MOST BELOVED ROMANCES—a warm, moving story of two cultures in conflict and two hearts in love.

Matt Thorne had come to his sister's rural inn to recover from an injury, far from the city and his fast-paced life as an emergency room physician. Drifting between sleep and wakefulness, Matt didn't trust his eyes when he saw the young woman who sat at his bedside in her plain cotton dress and apron, her chestnut hair tucked demurely beneath a white bonnet, like a beautiful vision from the past century.

Sarah Troyer had been warned about the womanizing Dr. Thorne, but nothing prepared her for the shiver of desire that shook her to her core when she gazed at him. Though her life was bound by the simple Amish way, Sarah had always longed for the world outside. Sarah was willing to allow herself a brief, secret adventure in the arms of a forbidden man. But she hadn't counted on Matt's passionate love—a love that would not let go, a love that could cost them both everything they knew. . . .

"You are to stay in bed."
"My favorite place to be—provided I'm not alone."
"Well, you're sure going to be alone here," she said tartly, finding a little bit of the sass that had always bought her a

glower of disapproval from her father. With this man it only seemed to generate more of his teasing humor.

He chuckled weakly, wincing a bit and laying a hand gingerly against the white bandage that swathed his ribs. "Oh, come on, Sarah. Have pity on a poor cripple. You're not really going to make me stay in bed all alone, are you?"

"You bet." She nodded resolutely.

"Then I'm afraid I'm going to have to make a speedy recovery. I can't stand the idea of having a beautiful nurse and not being able to chase her around the bed."

Beautiful. Sarah did her best to ignore his compliment. To accept a compliment was to accept credit for God's doing. It was *Hochmut*—pride—a sin. She didn't need to be charged with any more of them than she already had. So she brushed aside the warm glow that threatened to blossom inside her and decided to match him teasing for teasing. "The shape you're in, I'll have no trouble getting away."

Matt gave her a look. "Gee, don't spare my feelings here, Sarah. Lay it on the line."

"I'm sorry," she said, having the grace to blush. "I'm much too forthright. It's always getting me into trouble."

"Really?" Matt chuckled. "I can't imagine you in trouble."

"Ach, me, I'm in trouble all the time," she admitted, rolling her eyes. A secretive little Mona Lisa smile teased her lips as she stepped closer to the bed.

A sweet, warm feeling flooded through Matt. It wasn't exactly lust. It was . . . liking. Sarah Troyer was beguiling him with her innocence, and he would have bet she didn't have the vaguest idea she was doing it. "What kinds of things get you in trouble?"

Her smile faded and she glanced away. *Wishing for things I shouldn't want. Wanting things I can't have.* But her thoughts remained unspoken. The flush that stained her cheeks with color now was from guilt. She was what she was, and she should be grateful for the things she had, she reminded herself, tamping down the longing that sprang eternal in her soul. Like weeds in a garden, her father would say, they must be torn out by the roots. Somehow, she had never had the heart to dig that deep and tear out all her dreams.

She realized with a start that Matt was watching her, waiting for an answer. "Neglecting my work gets me into trouble," she said quietly, eyes downcast to keep him from seeing any other answers that might be revealed by those too-honest mirrors of her true feelings. "I had best go down and see to making you some supper."

"In a minute," Matt murmured, catching her by the wrist as she turned to go. Her skin was soft and cool beneath his fingertips, like the finest silk. He'd always had an especially acute sense of touch, and now he picked up the delicate beating of Sarah's pulse as if it were pounding like a jackhammer. He wondered if she would even know what a jackhammer was, and he marveled again at how untouched she seemed to him. He felt like the most jaded cynic in comparison.

She would know nothing about the kind of violence that had disrupted his life. Street gangs and drug wars and inner-city desperation were the trappings of another world, a world far removed from farm life and people who disdained automobiles as being too worldly.

He wanted to ask Sarah about the shadows that had crossed her face an instant before she had answered his question. He found he wanted to know all about her. He wrote it off as a combination of boredom and natural curiosity, and conveniently ignored the fact that he was not usually so curious about the deep, dark secrets of the women in his life.

It wasn't that he was so self-absorbed, he didn't care. It was more a matter of practicality. His career took precedence over all else in his life, and it left little time or energy for deep relationships. He wore his title of hospital Romeo with ease and good humor, and thought of all-consuming romantic love in only the most abstract of ways. So when Sarah Troyer turned back toward him, her eyes as blue as twin lakes under the sun and as round as quarters, he put the jolt in his chest down to a reawakening libido and counted himself lucky to be among the living.

"I think I might need a little help getting up," he said, his voice a notch huskier than usual.

"I think you might need to get your hearing checked," Sarah said breathlessly. She extricated her arm from his hold and stepped out of his reach, absently rubbing her wrist as if she could erase the tingling his touch had roused. "You are not to get out of bed."

"Fine," Matt said, scowling. "Don't help me. I'll manage."

Taking great care to move slowly, he eased his legs over the edge of the bed and waited for his head to stop swimming. Out of deference to Sarah's undoubtedly delicate sensibilities, he pulled the black-and-purple quilt around himself toga-style, then he took as deep a breath as his taped ribs would allow and rose.

The earth tilted drunkenly beneath his feet and he staggered forward in an effort to keep himself from falling. The quilt dropped away as he reached out to grab onto something—anything—to steady himself. The "something" his hands settled on gasped and squirmed. His eyes locked on Sarah's for an instant, an instant full of shock, surprise, and the unmistakable sparks of attraction, then they both went down in a tangle of arms and legs, quilt, and ankle-length cotton skirt.

Sarah gave a squeal as she landed on her back. Matt groaned as he came down on top of her, pain digging into his ribs and pounding through his head. A red-hot arrow of it shot down his left leg and a blissful blackness began to descend over him, beckoning him toward the peace of unconsciousness, but he fought it off. He sucked a breath in through his teeth, held it, expelled it slowly, all the while willing himself to remain in the land of the living.

After a moment that seemed like an eternity, the pain

receded. He slowly became aware of the feminine form cushioning his body. There really was a woman under all those clothes, he thought, mentally taking inventory of full breasts and shapely legs. His hands had settled at the curve of her waist, and he let his fingers trace the angles of it. She was trim but womanly. *Very* womanly, he thought, groaning again, but this time in appreciation as she shifted beneath him, and the points of her nipples grazed his chest through the cotton of her gown.

"Are you all right?" Sarah asked, trying to sound concerned as a whole array of other feelings assaulted her—panic, desire, guilt. Matt Thorne was pressed against the whole length of her, and while there might have been some question about his health, there was certainly no question about his gender. She squirmed frantically beneath him, only managing to come into even more intimate contact with him. She had automatically grabbed him as they had fallen, and now she found her hands gripping the powerful muscles of his upper arms. His skin was smooth and hot to the touch, and her fingers itched to explore more of it. How she managed to push the thought from her head and speak was beyond her. "Are you injured?"

"Me?" Matt said dreamily, his thick lashes drifting down as his smile curved his mouth upward. "I'm in heaven."

SMOKE EYES
by Maureen Reynolds

"a very HOT writer. . . . guaranteed to take
readers to new heights of sensuality."
—*Romantic Times*

*He was a dark–eyed captain home from the wild
sea . . . she was the exquisite treasure he had come
to plunder. . . .*

With her gray eyes flashing fire, Katherine Flynn was torn between
anger and breathless awe at the sight of her old childhood friend. A
respected and dedicated doctor in a small Colorado town, she'd
worked hard to overcome the double prejudice she faced as a woman
and an Arapaho half–breed. Why had Zach come back after all these
years? Still one look at the dangerous, steel-muscled man he'd become
was enough to set her body burning with forbidden desire—and to
persuade her to risk everything for one stolen moment in a handsome
brigand's arms.

In the following scene, Katherine is fetched by a deputy to come
to the jail to attend to an injured prisoner. . . .

   Everyone who had been in the store followed Katherine
and Tom to the jail, jabbering excitedly up the front steps
and clumping behind them. When Katherine entered the
jail, she gasped at the sight of the sheriff with his gun trained
on the prisoner in the first cell. She did not even let her gaze
slide toward the prisoner, keeping it fixed on the gun instead.

"Good Lord, Sheriff!" she said. "Is that necessary?"

"He's dangerous, Doc. An animal! Lookit what he did to Tom there."

"He can't hurt you behind bars," Katherine said. Though she had not yet looked at the prisoner, she could feel his presence, big and dark and menacing. She sensed his gaze on her, and felt a waiting stillness in the air, as if they'd caged a tiger that was getting ready to pounce.

"Sheriff," she said, "let me into the cell so I can see if he needs suturing."

The sheriff jerked the pistol toward the keys hanging on the wall behind the desk, and Tom went to fetch them.

"You so much as *look* at her crossways," the sheriff warned the prisoner, "an' I'll blow yer head clear off."

The sheriff pulled back the trigger, and Katherine heard the sharp click of a cartridge. The prisoner made a low sound in his throat, and she turned to him in time to see him whirl around and stare out the small barred window at the rear of the cell. He was tall and lean with incredibly wide shoulders packed with iron muscle. Even beneath the fabric of his rough striped shirt she could see those hard muscles shift and ripple. Awed by the size of him, she let her gaze drift over his broad back, down to his lean waist, and lower, to where his black trousers clung to his form so intimately she could see the slight hollows in his tight, hard buttocks. A strange sensation flickered through her, and she quickly looked up at his rock-hard profile.

Tom unlocked the door and, with the sheriff muttering something behind her, Katherine stepped into the cell. The prisoner ignored her.

"Sir," she said, "would you please come sit on the bunk so I can tend to you?"

Slowly, he turned to face her. Because the light was behind him, she could not make out his features, but there was no denying his mocking tone. "Sir?" he repeated. "Have you forgotten, madam, that I am in this cell because I've been accused of murder?"

Katherine turned briskly to set her bag on the bunk and open it. She heard his booted heels strike the stone floor— once, twice—then he was beside her, and she could smell him, earthy and male.

With trembling fingers she rummaged through her bag while the big stranger settled himself on the bunk, long legs sprawled wide. After removing her coat, she laid her instruments on a rickety chair. When she turned to the prisoner, her heart stopped. Somehow she had ended up standing between his wide-spread legs.

She glanced at his face, still shadowed in the poorly lit cell. Quickly she averted her eyes to the opened skin under a lock of thick black hair, matted with blood. As she moved closer to him she could almost feel his amused gaze on her face. She ignored it and pushed his hair aside to reveal the wound near his temple, still trickling blood. "You'll need a stitch or two," she said.

He didn't answer, but she was aware that he watched her face with a quiet intensity. She kept her own eyes lowered as she swiftly threaded a needle with a length of catgut. Stepping close again, she lifted the needle and told him to keep still. He didn't flinch as the needle pierced his skin, but he did speak.

"Are you going to tell that inept excuse for a lawman to take his gun off my head, Smoke Eyes?"

Katherine jolted as if someone had put a cattle prod to her flesh. The needle dropped from her nerveless fingers as she stared at the man as if she'd seen a ghost. And she may as well have, she thought, her breath quickening. She blinked, then peered closely at his solemn face, her gaze running over his rugged features as if he might vanish in a moment. *Smoke Eyes*. Only the folks she'd grown up with knew her by her Arapaho name.

With her heart in her throat, she lifted a hand and touched her fingers to his jaw. Black eyes, black hair. A hard, handsome face. She'd known a boy that fit that description, and had last seen him eleven years ago. Her mouth was suddenly dry, her throat aching as she opened her mouth to whisper one disbelieving word. "Zach?"

OFFICIAL RULES TO WINNERS CLASSIC SWEEPSTAKES

No Purchase necessary. To enter the sweepstakes follow instructions found elsewhere in this offer. You can also enter the sweepstakes by hand printing your name, address, city, state and zip code on a 3" x 5" piece of paper and mailing it to: Winners Classic Sweepstakes, P.O. Box 785, Gibbstown, NJ 08027. Mail each entry separately. Sweepstakes begins 12/1/91. Entries must be received by 6/1/93. Some presentations of this sweepstakes may feature a deadline for the Early Bird prize. If the offer you receive does, then to be eligible for the Early Bird prize your entry must be received according to the Early Bird date specified. Not responsible for lost, late, damaged, misdirected, illegible or postage due mail. Mechanically reproduced entries are not eligible. All entries become property of the sponsor and will not be returned.

Prize Selection/Validations: Winners will be selected in random drawings on or about 7/30/93, by VENTURA ASSOCIATES, INC., an independent judging organization whose decisions are final. Odds of winning are determined by total number of entries received. Circulation of this sweepstakes is estimated not to exceed 200 million. Entrants need not be present to win. All prizes are guaranteed to be awarded and delivered to winners. Winners will be notified by mail and may be required to complete an affidavit of eligibility and release of liability which must be returned within 14 days of date of notification or alternate winners will be selected. Any guest of a trip winner will also be required to execute a release of liability. Any prize notification letter or any prize returned to a participating sponsor, Bantam Doubleday Dell Publishing Group, Inc., its participating divisions or subsidiaries, or VENTURA ASSOCIATES, INC. as undeliverable will be awarded to an alternate winner. Prizes are not transferable. No multiple prize winners except as may be necessary due to unavailability, in which case a prize of equal or greater value will be awarded. Prizes will be awarded approximately 90 days after the drawing. All taxes, automobile license and registration fees, if applicable, are the sole responsibility of the winners. Entry constitutes permission (except where prohibited) to use winners' names and likenesses for publicity purposes without further or other compensation.

Participation: This sweepstakes is open to residents of the United States and Canada, except for the province of Quebec. This sweepstakes is sponsored by Bantam Doubleday Dell Publishing Group, Inc. (BDD), 666 Fifth Avenue, New York, NY 10103. Versions of this sweepstakes with different graphics will be offered in conjunction with various solicitations or promotions by different subsidiaries and divisions of BDD. Employees and their families of BDD, its division, subsidiaries, advertising agencies, and VENTURA ASSOCIATES, INC., are not eligible.

Canadian residents, in order to win, must first correctly answer a time limited arithmetical skill testing question. Void in Quebec and wherever prohibited or restricted by law. Subject to all federal, state, local and provincial laws and regulations.

Prizes: The following values for prizes are determined by the manufacturers' suggested retail prices or by what these items are currently known to be selling for at the time this offer was published. Approximate retail values include handling and delivery of prizes. Estimated maximum retail value of prizes: 1 Grand Prize ($27,500 if merchandise or $25,000 Cash); 1 First Prize ($3,000); 5 Second Prizes ($400 each); 35 Third Prizes ($100 each); 1,000 Fourth Prizes ($9.00 each) ; 1 Early Bird Prize ($5,000); Total approximate maximum retail value is $50,000. Winners will have the option of selecting any prize offered at level won. Automobile winner must have a valid driver's license at the time the car is awarded. Trips are subject to space and departure availability. Certain black-out dates may apply. Travel must be completed within one year from the time the prize is awarded. Minors must be accompanied by an adult. Prizes won by minors will be awarded in the name of parent or legal guardian.

For a list of Major Prize Winners (available after 7/30/93): send a self-addressed, stamped envelope entirely separate from your entry to: Winners Classic Sweepstakes Winners, P.O. Box 825, Gibbstown, NJ 08027. Requests must be received by 6/1/93. DO NOT SEND ANY OTHER CORRESPONDENCE TO THIS P.O. BOX.